"I think you're smart and brave and amazing. Which is why I can't do this."

"Do what?"

"Pretend to be the kind of man you deserve. A good father... A good husband... A good son... Name any kind of relationship, and it's one I've already failed. I don't know what this is between us, but I don't want it to be— I don't want you to be one more person I fail."

Debbie was right, Rory realized. He really did think he was saving her from herself. His noble effort was something she might have admired if she wasn't so tempted to smack him upside the head.

"You only fail when you stop trying. You haven't stopped trying with your father and you won't stop trying with Hannah. Not because that's the kind of man I deserve but because that's the kind of man you are. And as for the two of us..." She sucked in a deep breath. "I know how this ends, Jamison. With you and Hannah saying goodbye. Whether we spend those days together or not, that doesn't change. Whether you kiss me right now or not, that doesn't change. So the only question is...why *not* kiss me?"

* * *

HILLCREST HOUSE: Destination...romance

Dear Reader,

Welcome to Hillcrest House: destination...romance!

Who doesn't love a happily-ever-after? It's one of the things that has always drawn me to reading (and writing!) romance novels. Knowing that no matter how bad things get around chapter seven, by the end of the book, everything will have worked out. Life may not be perfect; there will still be struggles. But the hero and heroine will have found a lasting love and their own happy ending.

That kind of happy ending is one Rory McClaren has believed in since she was a little girl. The chance to work as a wedding coordinator at Hillcrest House, her family's Victorian hotel, has only strengthened her faith that she will find the man of her dreams...and she is certain that man is *not* corporate lawyer Jamison Porter!

Single father Jamison Porter has serious doubts about standing up as the best man in his friend's wedding. He's the last person who should be giving a toast to love and marriage. He's far too cynical and too jaded to count on happily-ever-after lasting beyond the honeymoon. So why is he having such a hard time getting bright and beautiful Rory off his mind?

With a little help from Jamison's daughter, who thinks Rory is a fairy-tale princess and fairy godmother all rolled into one, Rory and Jamison soon find their own (you guessed it) happily-ever-after.

I hope you enjoy this trip to Hillcrest House and that you will watch for the next two books in the series. These couples might not be looking for love, but at a gorgeous Victorian hotel that promises romance and happily-ever-after, what else can they say but "I do"?

Happy reading!

Stacy Connelly

The Best Man Takes a Bride

Stacy Connelly

HARLEQUIN® SPECIAL EDITION

Recycling programs
for this product may
not exist in your area.

ISBN-13: 978-1-335-46563-4

The Best Man Takes a Bride

Copyright © 2018 by Stacy Cornell

Printed in U.S.A.

Stacy Connelly has dreamed of publishing books since she was a kid, writing stories about a girl and her horse. Eventually, boys made it onto the pages as she discovered a love of romance and the promise of happily-ever-after. When she is not lost in the land of make-believe, Stacy lives in Arizona with her three spoiled dogs. She loves to hear from readers at stacyconnelly@cox.net or stacyconnelly.com.

Books by Stacy Connelly

Harlequin Special Edition

The Pirelli Brothers

His Secret Son
Romancing the Rancher
Small-Town Cinderella
Daddy Says, "I Do!"
Darcy and the Single Dad
Her Fill-In Fiancé

Temporary Boss...Forever Husband
The Wedding She Always Wanted
Once Upon a Wedding
All She Wants for Christmas

Visit the Author Profile page at Harlequin.com for more titles.

To all my fellow romance readers out there
and the ongoing search for happily-ever-after...
in (and out) of the pages of a romance novel!

Chapter One

This was going to be a disaster.

Jamison Porter eyed the dress shop with a sense of dread. Early-morning sunshine warmed the back of his neck and glinted off the gilded lettering on the plate glass window. Frilly dresses decorated with layer after layer of lace and ribbons and bows draped the mannequins on display, a small sample of the froth and satin inside. All of it girlie, delicate and scary as hell.

The forecast promised a high in the low seventies, but Jamison could already feel himself breaking into a sweat.

He swallowed hard against the sense of impending doom and fought the urge to jump in his SUV and floor it back to San Francisco. Back to his office and his black walnut barricade of a desk, matching bookshelves lined with heavy law books, and rich leather chairs. All of it masculine, substantial—the one place where Jamison never questioned his decisions, never doubted his every move—

He felt a tug at his hand and looked down at his four-year-old daughter's upturned face. Big brown eyes stared back at him. "I wanna go home now."

Never felt so useless as he did when he was with Hannah.

His daughter's barely brushed blond curls tilted to one side in a crooked ponytail. Her mismatched green T-shirt and pink shorts, both nearing a size too small, were testimony to the crying fit that ended their last attempt at clothes shopping. Jamison at least took some small comfort that Hannah had been the one to leave the store in tears, and not him. Because there were times…

Like now, when he didn't even know which home Hannah was referring to. Back to Hillcrest House, the hotel where they'd be staying for the next couple of weeks? Back to his town house in San Francisco? To her grandparents' place? To the house where she'd been living with her mother…

"I know, Hannah Banana," he said, fighting another shaft of disappointment when the once-loved nickname failed to bring a smile to her face. "But we can't go home yet," he added as he set aside the question of where his daughter called home for another time. "We're here to meet Lindsay, remember? She's the lady who's getting married to my friend Ryder, and she wants you to be her flower girl."

Hannah scraped the toe of a glittery tennis shoe along a crack in the sidewalk. "I don't want to."

Her lack of interest in playing a role in Lindsay Brookes's wedding to Ryder Kincaid didn't bother Jamison as much as her patented response did. Not because of all the things Hannah didn't want, but because of the one thing she did.

The bell above the shop's frosted-glass door rang as the

bride stepped outside. Dressed in gray slacks and a sleeveless peach top with her dark blond hair caught back in a loose bun, a smile lit Lindsay's pretty face. "Hey, you made it! Not that I thought you wouldn't." She waved a hand, the solitaire in her engagement ring flashing in the sunlight. "I mean, it isn't like any place around here is hard to find!"

Ryder had told Jamison his hometown near the Northern California coastline was small, and he hadn't exaggerated. Victorian buildings lined either side of Main Street and made up the heart of downtown. Green-and-white awnings snapped in the late-summer breeze, adding to the welcome of nodding yellow snapdragons, purple pansies and white petunias in the brick planters outside the shops. Couples strolled arm in arm, their laughing kids racing ahead to dart into the diner down the street or into the sweet-smelling café across the way.

It was all quaint and old-fashioned, postcard perfect and roughly that same size. Jamison figured it had taken less than five minutes to see all Clearville had to offer even while obeying the slower-than-slow posted speed limit. "No trouble. Didn't even need to use the GPS."

Finding the shop had been easy. Making himself step one foot inside, that was a different story.

"Good thing," Lindsay said with a laugh, "since cell coverage can be pretty spotty around here."

Jamison fought back a groan. In a true effort to focus on Hannah and leave work behind, he hadn't brought along his laptop. But he'd been counting on being able to use his phone to read emails and download any documents too urgent to wait for his return. "How does anyone get things done around here?" he grumbled under his breath.

She lifted a narrow shoulder in a shrug. "Disconnecting is tough at first, but before long, you find you don't miss it at all."

"Can't say I plan to be in town long enough to get used to anything," he replied as the driver of an SUV crawling down Main Street called out to Lindsay and the two women exchanged a quick wave.

And despite his own words, Jamison couldn't help thinking that, back in San Francisco, had a driver shouted and stuck an arm out the window, the gesture wouldn't have been so friendly.

"That's too bad. Clearville's a great town. A wonderful place to raise a family," she added with a warm glance at Hannah, who dropped her gaze and retreated even farther behind his back.

So different from the adventurous toddler he remembered…

He sucked in a deep breath as he tried to focus on whatever Lindsay was saying.

"But why don't we get started? I'm here for my final fitting, and I've picked out some of the cutest flower girl dresses. Our colors are burgundy and gold, but I think that would be too strong a palette for Hannah since she's so fair. Instead I've been leaning toward a cream taffeta with a sash at the waist—"

Catching herself, Lindsay offered a sheepish smile. "Sorry, Ryder's already warned me I tend to go into wedding overload on even the most unsuspecting victim. The other day, I talked a poor waitress's ear off and all she asked was if I wanted dessert. If there's something else you need to do, you don't have to stay—"

"No! Daddy, don't go!" Hannah's hands tightened in a death grip around his as she pressed closer to his side.

Lindsay's expression morphed into one of sympathy that Jamison had seen too many times and had grown to despise over the past two months.

But not as much as he hated the tears in his daughter's

eyes. "I'm not going anywhere," he vowed, disappointed but not surprised when his promise didn't erase the worry wrinkling her pale eyebrows.

"Pinkie promise?" she finally asked, holding out the tiny, delicate digit.

Jamison didn't hesitate as Hannah wrapped him around her finger. Love welled up inside him along with the painful awareness of how many times he'd let her down in her short life. His voice was gruff as he replied, "Pinkie promise."

"Your daddy can stay with you the whole time," Lindsay reassured Hannah gently. "I bet he can't wait to see you try on some pretty dresses."

Jamison had thought Hannah might enjoy being a flower girl, but the truth was, he didn't have a clue what would make his little girl happy anymore. Sweat started to gather at his temples along with the pressure of an oncoming headache. "Look, Lindsay, I appreciate you thinking of Hannah and wanting her to be part of the ceremony, but I don't—"

"Sorry I'm late!" The cheery voice interrupted Jamison's escape, and every muscle in his body tensed. That need to run raced through him once more, but his feet felt frozen in place. Still, he couldn't help turning to glance over his shoulder, bracing himself for the woman he could feel drawing closer.

The wedding coordinator.

Ryder and Lindsay had introduced them not long after he'd checked into the sprawling Victorian hotel. He'd been exhausted from fourteen-hour workdays, worn out from the long drive from San Francisco and far more overwhelmed by the idea of taking care of Hannah on his own than he dared admit even to himself.

That was the only logical explanation he'd been able

to come up with for why that first meeting with Rory McClaren had sent a lightning bolt straight through his chest. Her smile had stopped him dead in his tracks and her touch—nothing more than a simple handshake—had shot a rush of adrenaline through his system, jump-starting his heartbeat and sending it racing for the first time in... ever, it seemed.

But logical explanations failed him now. One look at Rory, and Jamison was blown away all over again.

Big blue eyes sparkled in a heart-shaped face framed by dark, shoulder-length hair. A fringe of bangs, thick lashes and arched eyebrows drew him even deeper into that gaze. A sprinkling of freckles across her nose kept her fair skin from being too perfect, and cherry-red lipstick highlighted a bright smile and a sexy mouth Jamison had no business thinking about again and again.

A white sundress stitched with red roses revealed more freckles scattered like gold dust across her delicate collarbones. The fitted bodice hugged the curves of her breasts and small waist before flaring to swish around her slender legs as she walked.

She looked as fresh and sunny as a summer's day, and Jamison almost had to squint when he looked at her, like he needed sunglasses to shield him from her stunning beauty.

He sure as hell needed some form of protection, some barrier to establish a safe distance from this woman and the unexpected, unwanted way she made him feel. If his disastrous marriage had taught him one lesson, it was that he far preferred being numb.

"Mr. Porter, nice to see you again."

Her smile was genuine, but Jamison couldn't imagine her words were true. He'd been abrupt the day before, unnerved by his reaction and bordering on rude. "Ms. McClaren. I didn't know you'd be joining us this morning."

"All part of Hillcrest House's service as an all-inclusive wedding venue," she said with a smile to Lindsay before turning that full wattage on Jamison. "But we are a hotel first and foremost, so I hope you enjoyed your first night under our roof."

He'd heard his share of come-ons in his lifetime. There was nothing the least bit seductive in her smile or her voice. But his imagination, as suddenly uncontrollable as his hormones, had him picturing an intimacy beyond sleeping under her roof and instead sleeping in her bed...

Jamison didn't know if his thoughts were written on his face, but whatever Rory saw had enough color blooming in her cheeks to rival the roses on her dress. Her lips parted on an inhaled breath, and Jamison felt drawn closer, captured by the moment as the awareness stretched between them until she dropped her gaze.

"And Hannah!"

That quickly, the enticing image was banished, but not the pained embarrassment lingering in its wake. He wasn't some gawky teenager lusting after the high school cheerleader. He was a grown man, a father...a father with a daughter he was terrified of failing—just like he had her mother.

"How are you this morning?" Undeterred by the lack of response, Rory's lyrical voice rose and fell, and Jamison didn't want to think about the slight tremor under the words. Didn't want to think she might be as affected as he was by the chemistry between them. "Do you like your room at the hotel? You know, the Bluebell has always been my favorite."

The Bluebell...

What kind of hotel designated their rooms by a type of flower?

"It's all part of Hillcrest's romantic charm," Rory had explained.

He had no need for romance or charm or bright-eyed brunettes. He wanted logic, order. He wanted the normalcy of sequential room numbers, for God's sake!

But the Bluebell was one of the hotel's few two-room suites and, while small, it offered a living space and tiny kitchenette. The comfortable room was subtly decorated in shades of blue and white.

If only it wasn't for the name…and the reminder of flowers that had him thinking far too often of Rory's dark-lashed, vibrant blue eyes.

"I like purple," Hannah answered, surprising him too much with her willingness to talk to a virtual stranger for him to point out bluebell wasn't a color.

"Me, too," Rory agreed as she caught on to his daughter's twist in the topic.

Hannah's forehead wrinkled. "You said you like blue."

"Actually, Hannah, rainbow is my favorite color…" The wedding coordinator bent at the waist so she and Hannah were almost eye to eye as she shared that piece of nonsense with the little girl. "That way I never have to pick just one."

A lock of her hair slid forward like a silken ribbon and curved around her breast. The dark strands were a stark contrast against the white fabric, but it was the similarities that had Jamison sucking in a deep breath. Soft cotton, soft hair, soft skin…

Realizing he was staring, he jerked his gaze away. Falling back on good manners now that good sense seemed to have deserted him, he ground out, "Hannah, you remember Ms. McClaren?"

His daughter nodded, her eyes too serious for her still-baby face as she peered up at the wedding coordinator. She wrapped her index finger in the hem of her shirt, holding on the same way she had to the pink-and-white blanket Jamison remembered her carrying with her everywhere when she was a toddler. "She's Miss Lindsay's fairy godmother."

Jamison blinked at Hannah's unexpected announcement. "She's… Oh, right." That was how Lindsay had introduced the woman. The bride had sung Rory McClaren's praises, complimenting her on finding the perfect music, the perfect flowers, the perfect menu—as if any of that attention to detail would lead to the perfect marriage.

Jamison knew better. He was cynical enough to wonder if Rory knew the same, but not cynical enough to believe it. Everything about her was too genuine, too hopeful for him to convince himself it was all for show. But even if the wedding coordinator believed what she was selling, that didn't mean Jamison was buying.

"She's not really a fairy godmother," he told his daughter firmly.

"Of course not," the dark-haired pixie said with a conspiring wink at the little girl, who gazed back with shy curiosity. "And you can call me Rory."

Jamison's jaw tightened. No doubt Rory thought the shared moment with Hannah was harmless, but the last thing he needed was for his daughter to put faith in fairy tales. Especially when the one thing Hannah wanted was the one thing no one—not even a fairy godmother, if such a thing existed—could give her.

Rory's smile faltered when she glanced up into his face. Straightening, she rallied by getting down to business and glancing between Lindsay and Hannah. "So, are we ready to start trying on some gorgeous dresses?"

"I can't wait!" Lindsay announced, clapping her hands in front of her as if trying to hold on to her excitement.

"I've picked out some of the cutest dresses, and you have got to help me decide which one to choose."

"That is what I'm here for. Anything you need, all you have to do is ask!"

And with statements like that, Jamison thought, was it any wonder Hannah thought the woman was some kind of fairy godmother? Even he half expected a magic wand to appear in the delicate hand she waved through the air.

Better to leave now before he—before *Hannah*—could get sucked any further into a belief in fairy tales and happily-ever-afters.

"About that. I think Hannah might be a little too young for all of this."

Lindsay sank back onto her heels, her earlier excitement leaking out of her. He wasn't a man to go back on his word, but he never should have agreed to have Hannah in the wedding in the first place. With his in-laws pointing out the need for a female influence in Hannah's life, he'd thought—hell, Jamison didn't know what he'd thought. But the whole idea was a mistake. "Trying on clothes isn't her idea of fun."

This time, though, the wedding coordinator's smile didn't dim in the least. If anything, an added spark came to her eyes. "The shopping gene hasn't kicked in yet?"

"I'm hoping it skips a generation."

Rory laughed as though he'd been joking, brightening her expression even more, like a spotlight showcasing a work of art. "You and all fathers everywhere."

It was a small thing—Rory categorizing him as a typical dad—but some of the pressure eased in his chest. Maybe it wasn't so obvious from the outside that he was at such a loss when it came to his own daughter. Best to quit while he was, if not ahead, then at least breaking even.

But before he could once again make his excuses, Rory

turned to Hannah. "Well, maybe Miss Lindsay can go first. What do you think, Hannah? Are you ready to help?"

"Ms. McClaren—"

"Why does she need help?" It was Hannah who interrupted this time, coming out from behind him far enough to look from Rory to Lindsay. "She's a grown-up, and big girls should be old enough to get dressed by themselves."

Jamison closed his eyes and wished for a sinkhole to open up in the sidewalk and swallow him whole at his words coming out of Hannah's mouth. *Crap.* Was that really how he sounded? So…condescending and demeaning?

"Hannah…" He'd only pulled out the big-girl card because Hannah was so filled with ideas of what she would do when she was older. Or at least she had been.

But if Rory was ready to take that "typical dad" title away from him and flag him with "worst father ever," she didn't let it show as she knelt down in front of his little girl. Close enough this time that he could have stroked her hair, as dark as Hannah's was light, and he shoved his free hand into his pocket before insanity had him reaching out…

"You know, Hannah," Rory was saying, her voice filled with that same touch of sharing a secret she'd conveyed earlier with that wink, "funny thing about being a big girl…sometimes we still need help."

As she spoke, she reached up and slipped the bright pink band from Hannah's hair. With a few quick swipes of her hands and without a comb or brush in sight, she had the little girl's curls contained in a smooth, well-centered ponytail. "Not a lot of help. Just a little, just enough to make things right."

To make things right… Jamison didn't have a clue how to go about making things right in his daughter's world. Especially not when he saw the open longing and amazement in Hannah's face as she reached up to touch her now-perfect ponytail.

"So what do you think?" Rory asked as she straightened, her full skirt swirling around her legs. The roses on her dress might have been embroidered, but somehow Jamison still caught a sweet, fresh scent, as if she'd risen from a bed of wildflowers. "Do you want to help Lindsay with her dress for the wedding?"

Hannah hesitated, and Jamison braced himself for the "I don't want to" response. Instead, she surprised him, nodding once and sliding a little farther out from behind him.

"And maybe, after Lindsay's done, we could find a dress for you. Just to try on—you know, like playing dress-up. And then you can put your everyday clothes back on, because who wants to wear dresses all the time?"

Hannah reached out and brushed her tiny hand over Rory's skirt. "You do."

Rory tilted her head to the side as she laughed. "You caught me. I do like wearing dresses. But not *all* the time."

Jamison might have only met the woman, but he already sensed how Rory's clothes—elegant and old-fashioned—suited her. He had a hard time picturing her in anything else.

Now, if he could only stop himself from picturing her wearing nothing at all…

Chapter Two

When Rory McClaren was five years old, she went through a princess phase. Her cousin Evie would likely say she never fully recovered from her belief in true love and happy endings and fascination with gorgeous ball gowns. Or the hidden longing to wear a tiara. On a Tuesday. Just for fun.

And while Rory had denied those longings throughout her adult life, her new position as wedding coordinator for Hillcrest House brought out every once-upon-a-time memory. She might have laughed it off when Lindsay Brookes had introduced her as a fairy godmother, but it was secretly how she viewed her job.

Of course, Rory also knew what Evie would say about that.

Coordinating weddings is a serious business, not a game of pretend. And Hillcrest House isn't a fairy-tale castle, no matter what you thought as a kid.

Neither she nor Evie had planned on this recent stay in Clearville, but the two of them were in this together—doing all they could to keep Hillcrest House running while their aunt was going through cancer treatments. Evie, a CPA, was handling the books and the staff while Rory was taking on a guest relations role as well as event planning for the venue.

So far, Lindsay Brookes had been a dream to work with, but her wedding to Ryder Kincaid came with some extra pressure. Not only did Rory consider Lindsay a friend, the pretty businesswoman also worked for Clearville's chamber of commerce. She was constantly promoting the small Northern California town and its businesses.

Rory wanted to prove all the brochures and promotions touting Hillcrest House as *the* all-inclusive wedding destination were as good as gold. The weight of responsibility pressed hard on her shoulders, but she was determined not to crumble.

She could certainly withstand a reticent best man and his shy flower girl daughter. Despite Jamison's claims that she didn't enjoy shopping, Hannah was gazing at the elegantly posed mannequins and racks of lacy dresses lining the walls of the small shop while her sharp-eyed father watched from close by.

With her tiny hands clasped behind her back, the little girl was clearly familiar with the phrase *look but don't touch*. Under her breath, she named off the color of each dress she came across in a singsong voice, and Rory didn't think it would take much to rid Hannah of her uncertainty in her role as a flower girl.

Her smile faded, though, when she caught sight of the storm clouds gathering in Jamison's eyes. Something told her erasing *his* concerns wouldn't be so easy.

Rory had hoped her initial impression of Ryder Kincaid's best friend had been a rush to judgment. She'd told herself that with a good night's sleep and a chance to relax and unwind, Jamison Porter would be a different man. A man she could handle with professional competence as she guided him through the duties of the best man from suggestions for a fun yet tasteful bachelor party to tips on a heartfelt toast.

But Jamison Porter was still every bit as intense and edgy as he had been the day before—and not a man easily handled.

It wasn't the first time Rory had been to this shop with a reluctant man in tow. Not every couple held to the superstition that the groom shouldn't see the bride in her gown. But none of the men had seemed so out of place as Jamison did. At over six feet, with rich chestnut hair and cool gray eyes, all rugged angles and sharp planes, he wore the tall, dark and handsome label to perfection. The airy dresses around him seemed as insubstantial in comparison as dandelion fluff, ready to disintegrate with a single puff of breath from his lips.

Not that Jamison Porter's lips were anything Rory should be thinking about...

"So, you're the best man," she said, cringing at the exuberant sound of her own voice.

"That's what Ryder tells me."

The hint of self-deprecating humor loosened a strand in the single father's too tightly laced personality. One that made him even more attractive than his classically handsome good looks.

But that was the last thing Rory needed. Their first meeting, as abrupt and tension filled as those moments had been, had sparked an awareness that had her thinking of the handsome single father far too often.

And just now while standing outside the bridal shop,

when she asked what she'd thought to be an innocent question about his first night at Hillcrest…

The intensity in his expression served notice there was nothing innocent about Jamison Porter. Everything about the man had Rory on high alert, raw nerve endings leaving her jumpy and out of sorts. Off her game at a time when she needed to be at her best.

Evie had taken a leave of absence from her job at the accounting firm to help out their aunt, confident they would hold her position for her, and had sublet her fabulous condo in Portland.

Whereas Rory—

Rory had nothing left. She couldn't afford *not* to come to Clearville. Back in LA, she had no boyfriend, no apartment, no job and a reputation left in tatters all thanks to her professional—and personal—failure.

Pushing thoughts of her short-lived interior design career aside, she focused on the most important aspects of the wedding.

"Ryder and Lindsay make such a wonderful couple. It's amazing the way they've reunited after so many years, and seeing them together… Well, they're crazy about each other."

Jamison gave a sound that wasn't quite a laugh. "*Crazy* is one word for it."

"And what word would you use?"

He paused for a moment, and Rory had a feeling he was searching for the least offensive description. "*Sudden,*" he said finally. "They just got engaged."

"True, but they've known each other since high school." Lindsay had filled Rory in on the couple's history, how she had been a shy bookworm with a huge crush on the popular quarterback. "They went their separate ways after graduation, but from what Lindsay says, she never stopped loving Ryder."

And while Ryder had gone on to marry another woman, Rory had no doubt he was in love with his future bride.

"She's a wonderful person. A great mother..."

The dark clouds in Jamison's eyes started flashing lightning and Rory's voice trailed away as she realized that was one box she shouldn't have opened. Unable to leave well enough alone, she couldn't help asking, "Have you met Robbie?"

He gave a quick nod. "I have."

"He's a great kid."

"One Ryder didn't even know about until a few months ago."

Rory sucked in a startled breath. Okay, so Jamison was breaking out the big guns to take on the elephant in the room. Fortunately, the curtain to the dressing room opened and Lindsay stepped out before he had time to reload.

Hannah's breathless voice broke the silence that followed. "You look beautiful."

This was the first time Rory had seen Lindsay in her wedding dress, and she couldn't hold back a whisper of her own. "Oh, Lindsay. Hannah is right. That dress is perfect."

Having worked on the flowers, the music and the table settings for the reception, Rory knew Lindsay had an elegant, timeless vision for the wedding, so it was no surprise her dress reflected that same taste.

The sheath-style gown was gorgeous in its simplicity; lace sleeves capped a straight column of white satin, and a hint of beadwork decorated the bodice and the lace insert that veed out into a modest train.

Lindsay gave a self-conscious laugh as she glanced at the silent member of the group. "It's not bad luck for the best man to see the bride in her gown, is it?"

To his credit, Jamison tipped his head at Lindsay. "You make a beautiful bride."

Lindsay blushed at the compliment, but while the words were right, Rory knew in her heart Jamison thought Ryder and Lindsay getting married was wrong.

A gentle tug on her skirt distracted Rory from the troubling thought. "Miss Rory, is it my turn to dress like a princess?"

She smiled down at Hannah. She was an adorable little girl with a riot of blond curls, big brown eyes and a shyness that tugged at Rory's heart.

But it was the expression on Jamison's face that had grabbed hold and wouldn't let go. A mix of love and uncertainty that held him frozen in place, as if he, too, were bound by the *look, don't touch* mantra.

"It sure is, sweetie," Rory said, injecting a positive note into her voice though she didn't know which of the Porters needed her encouragement more. "Miss Lindsay has a whole bunch of dresses for you to try on." Tilting her head in the direction of the changing room, Rory asked Jamison, "Do you want…"

Looking torn between Daddy duty and a man's typical reaction of running as far as he could from anything girlie, he said, "I, um, think I'll wait out here."

"What do you think, Hannah?" Rory asked when the little girl hesitated. "See, your daddy wants the princess dresses to be a surprise, so he'll wait in that chair over there."

Like father, like daughter. Hannah looked indecisively from her father to the curtained dressing room and back again. Finally her blond head bounced in a nod. "You wait there, Daddy, and no peeking."

Rory wouldn't have thought Jamison Porter could look any more uncomfortable than he had two seconds ago, but his daughter's instructions for him not to go peeking into the women's dressing room had a slight flush darkening his cheeks.

Rory fought to hide a smile, but judging by the narrowing of Jamison's eyes, she didn't succeed.

Biting the inside of her lip, she shot a stern look in his direction. "You heard the girl, Mr. Porter. No peeking."

For a split second, their eyes met, and Rory's smile faded as something electric and powerful passed between them. Heat flared in Jamison's eyes, a warning beacon, and she swallowed hard. He might not have looked behind the curtain, but when it came to her attraction to him, Rory feared he saw way too much.

The jingle of metal rings cut through Jamison's relentless pacing, and he glanced over in time to see Rory slip through the curtain.

The one his little girl had warned him not to peek behind. His faced started to heat again at the thought. Not because his own kid made him out to sound like some kind of Peeping Tom—she was only four, after all. But because of the moment that had followed.

The moment when Rory had echoed his daughter's words and his gaze had locked on hers and there'd been nothing—nothing—in his power that could keep him from mentally pulling back that curtain and picturing Rory McClaren wearing something far less than the old-fashioned dresses she favored.

Judging by the way her eyes had widened, she'd known it.

Clearing his throat, he asked, "Is Hannah—"

"She's fine. The seamstress is taking some measurements, and Hannah wanted me to make sure you're still waiting for her. She was a little nervous at first, but I think she's getting into the spirit of things. So, please..." She nodded her head at the waiting chair. "Sit down and relax."

He all but glared at the floral-print cushions that might as well have been covered with sharp thorns. Without some outlet for his excess energy, he'd likely explode. "Relaxing doesn't come easy to me."

"Really?" Rory drawled.

"That obvious, is it?" He supposed he shouldn't have been surprised. Maintaining a single-minded focus and blocking out the world around him had been a reflex since he was a kid.

His parents' divorce—hell, their entire marriage—had been a battlefield, his childhood collateral damage. The fights, the cold silences, the endless digs when the other wasn't around—Jamison had hated it all.

That volatile home life had made Jamison even more determined to keep the peace in his own marriage. He'd worked hard to give Monica everything she could need, everything she could want, everything she'd asked for and more.

And none of it had been enough to make her—or their marriage—happy.

Monica had always complained about the long hours he put in. Of course, Monica had complained about so many things that work became even more of a refuge.

A sweet giggle came from behind the curtain, and Rory murmured, "She's a beautiful little girl."

The innocent comment slammed through him. He needed to spend this time away from work with his daughter. He needed to find a way to reconnect, but he was at a loss to know how. And it galled him, he had to admit, how easily, how naturally Rory related to Hannah when for him it was all such a struggle.

"Thank you," he said stiffly, wishing he could take more

credit for the amazing little person Hannah was. But she even looked like Monica, a tiny carbon copy of his blond-haired, doe-eyed wife.

"She'll make an adorable flower girl," Rory said.

"I'm sure she will," Jamison said. "I'm just not sure about this whole wedding thing."

Rory cocked a questioning eyebrow. "The *whole* wedding?" she asked.

"Hannah's role in it," he amended, knowing he'd already said too much.

"I can see how she'd be nervous, walking down the aisle in front of all those people. But you'll be standing at Ryder's side, so all she has to do is keep her eyes on you, knowing you'll be watching her the whole way, and she'll do fine."

"You make it sound so easy."

"I have faith," she said lightly.

Of course she did. The Hillcrest wedding coordinator had faith, hope and light shining out of her. "Still, it's a lot of pressure to put on a little kid."

"Oh, I wasn't talking about Hannah. My faith is in you."

"In me?" Jamison echoed. "Why would you—" why would *anyone* "—put your faith in me?"

"Because I see the trust Hannah has in you. All you have to do is show her you'll be there for her, and she'll find the courage and confidence to move forward all on her own."

All you have to do is be there for her. Little did Rory know how seldom he'd been there for Hannah during her short life. First because of how hard he'd been working, and then because of Monica... But now he, as Hannah's only parent, was responsible for her health and happiness.

The weight of that responsibility pressed on Jamison's chest until he struggled to breathe. And he couldn't help wondering if his in-laws were right and if they weren't so much better equipped to raise Hannah…

"Ever think maybe you put too much faith in people?" he asked Rory, his voice rougher than necessary and so out of place in this shop filled with feminine softness.

"Sometimes," she admitted, surprising him with the candid answer. "And sometimes they let me down."

"Rory—" A hint of sadness clouded her beautiful features. And that restless energy inside him changed into an urge to close the distance between them, to pull her into his arms and wipe the lingering shadows from her blue eyes…

"Daddy, look!" His daughter's excited voice broke the moment, saving him from making a huge mistake, as she popped out from the dressing room. "It's a real princess dress! Just for me."

She giggled as she spun in a circle, the cream-colored lacy skirt flaring out around her tiny legs and glittery sneakers. The happy sound only magnified the ache, the guilt, pressing down on his chest. When was the last time he'd heard Hannah laugh?

"Just for you, Hannah," he vowed.

From now on, everything was just for his daughter.

Because if there was one thing he'd already done far too many times, it was let the females in his life down.

So despite the attraction, despite the knowing, tender look in the wedding coordinator's gaze, Jamison was going to keep his distance.

Chapter Three

"Oh, my gosh! Didn't Hannah look so cute?"

Seated at a wrought iron bistro table outside the café, Rory smiled as she listened to Lindsay describe every detail on the flower girl's dress. Not that she minded. The time with the sweet little girl was still playing through Rory's thoughts, as well.

Which was much better than thinking of the girl's not-so-sweet but undeniably hot father...

The bride-to-be's recitation stopped on a sigh as she paused to take a bite of a double-chocolate muffin. "Why did you bring me here?" she demanded. "That was supposed to be my final fitting, and after eating this dessert, I'm going to need to go back and have the seams let out at least two inches."

Eyeing Lindsay's slender frame, Rory laughed. "I think you're safe, and besides, we're splitting, remember?" she asked before breaking off a piece of the moist top rising above the sparkling pink wrapper. She gave a sigh of her own as rich chocolate melted in her mouth.

"Perfect, so the seams will only need to be let out one inch." Despite the complaint, Lindsay went in for another bite.

"You have nothing to worry about. Ryder is going to take one look at you walking down the aisle and be blown away."

The other woman smiled, but as she wiped her fingers on a napkin, Rory could see her heart wasn't in it. "Hey, everything okay? I know how busy you've been between the wedding and the benefit next week."

As part of her job promoting Clearville and its businesses, Lindsay was helping Jarrett Deeks with a rodeo at the local fairgrounds. The benefit was aimed at raising funds and awareness for the former rodeo star's horse rescue.

"Everything's on track. Jarrett lined up enough cowboys to compete, and local vendors have been amazing about donating their time and part of the proceeds from their booths." Despite the positive words, worry knit her dark blond brows, and she crumpled the napkin in her fist.

"So then what's wrong…and what can I do to help?" Lindsay was a Hillcrest bride, but she was also a friend. "Whatever you need, I'm here for you."

"You might wish you hadn't made that promise."

"I never make promises I don't keep," Rory vowed, her thoughts drifting back to her ex, Peter, and his many, many broken promises, but she shoved the memories away.

"Okay then," Lindsay exhaled a deep breath. "Here goes… It's Jamison. He and Ryder have known each other for years, and I can tell by how Ryder talks how close they are. He's already told me there's nothing he wouldn't do for Jamison, and I'm sure Jamison feels the same."

The last part was said with enough worry for unease to worm its way into Rory's stomach. "And what do you think Jamison's going to do?"

"I'm probably being paranoid. But my relationship with Ryder… Well, let's just say we didn't get off to the best start." The bride gave a shaky laugh at the understatement behind those words.

Rory might have moved to Clearville recently, but her frequent visits as a teenager had given her a taste of small-town life. Everyone knew everyone's business. Which was why it was still something of a shock among the local gossips that Lindsay Brookes had managed to keep her son's—Ryder's son's—paternity a secret for so long.

"But the two of you are together now," Rory reassured her friend, "and that's all that matters."

She might not know the whole story of how Lindsay and Ryder had worked out a decade of differences, but she'd seen for herself how in love the couple was. The way Ryder looked at Lindsay—

Rory pushed aside the pinpricks of envy jabbing at her heart to embrace the positive. If Ryder and Lindsay could overcome such odds and find their way back to each other, then surely there was hope for her. True love was out there somewhere, but right now her focus was Hillcrest House and helping her aunt. Her own happily-ever-after would wait.

"I know. Things are going so well, but I can't shake this feeling that something's going to go wrong. Like I'm waiting for the other shoe to drop."

"And you think that shoe's a size-eleven Italian loafer?"

Lindsay laughed. "You noticed that, huh?"

"I think it's safe to say Jamison's strung a bit tight for a guy who's supposed to be on vacation."

And was it any wonder she was determined to ignore

the instant, unwanted attraction? If Rory had a type, she certainly didn't want it to be Jamison Porter. He was a corporate attorney, for heaven's sake! A shark in a suit when she was looking for more of a—a puppy.

Someone sweet, lovable…loyal. Someone willing to defend her and stay by her side.

"From what I've heard from Ryder, Jamison doesn't do vacations. Ryder really had to push him to take this time off. I guess Jamison has some big deal in the works, but I think if he would take a day or two to relax, it might give him a different perspective on the whole wedding and, well, on me."

"Lindsay, Ryder loves you. And as for Jamison, I think he and Ryder need to go out for a couple of beers and a game of pool over at the Clearville Bar and Grille. They can do the whole high-fiving, name-calling, competitive guy thing, and all will be well."

Even as she said the words, Rory had a hard time picturing Jamison Porter at the local sports bar. He seemed like her ex, Peter, who was more interested in being seen by the right people in the right places. But then again, so much about Peter had all been for show…

"And Ryder's asked, but Jamison won't go. He doesn't want to leave Hannah."

And *that* did not sound like Peter at all. Maybe Rory had been too quick in making her comparisons.

"She's had a hard time since the accident."

"Accident?"

Lindsay nodded, sympathy softening her pretty features. "A car accident a few months ago. Hannah sustained a mild concussion and a broken arm, but she was the lucky one. Her mother was killed instantly."

"Oh, no." That lost look she'd picked up on in Hannah… and in Jamison. Rory had assumed it was nothing more than a single dad on his own with his daughter, far away from the comforts of home. She should have realized it was something deeper… "Poor Hannah. And Jamison, to lose his wife."

"They were separated, and from what Ryder's said, things hadn't been right between them for a long time. But still…"

"I guess you can't blame him if he has his doubts about love and marriage."

"That's what Ryder keeps telling me. Not everything going on in the world revolves around our wedding."

"You're the bride, Lindsay. Everything *does* revolve around the wedding."

Lindsay dropped what was left of the mangled napkin on the table and leaned forward with a relieved smile. "I knew you'd understand, Rory! You're the best wedding coordinator ever, and I knew I could count on you to help."

Rory's eyes narrowed. "What exactly am I helping with?"

"Well, with Jamison, of course. I thought if you could show him around town, spend some time with him—"

"Wait! What?" she asked in alarm. "Why me?"

"You have such a way with people. Of keeping calm and helping them relax. Not to mention how taken Hannah is with you. You saw that, and I know Jamison did, too."

Yes, Rory had noticed Hannah's shy fascination. Knowing the little girl had lost her mother added a sense of heartbreak to the tiny fingers that had wrapped around her hand. But it wasn't enough to erase the memory of the dark, disapproving clouds brewing in Jamison's gray gaze.

She'd dealt with enough parental disapproval in her relationship with Peter to last a lifetime.

"I don't think that's such a good idea, Lindsay. With everything Hannah and Jamison must be going through—"

"That's why this is so perfect!" her friend insisted. "Back home they're surrounded by memories, but Clearville—and you—are a clean slate. I know this isn't some miracle fix for what they've lost. No one expects that. All I'm asking is for you to show them around town. Give them a tour of Hillcrest House. You're always saying how magical the place is."

"So no miracles required, just performing a little magic," Rory said wryly as she sank back in her chair. But she was already caving despite Jamison's disapproval, despite her own reluctance to spend time with a man who made her heart skip a beat even when he was frowning at her.

Because once upon a time, Rory had found magic at Hillcrest House, and while her belief might have wavered a time or two over the years, it had never left her.

And when she thought about Hannah and the seriousness in her big brown eyes, Rory couldn't help thinking that belief in happily-ever-after was what the little girl needed.

As for Jamison... Well, there was some magic Rory wasn't sure even a fairy godmother could perform.

As a corporate lawyer at Spears, Moreland and Howe, one of the most prestigious firms in San Francisco, Jamison Porter was at the top of his game. He was vying for a promotion that would make him the youngest junior partner in the firm's history. He had a track record of success and negotiated million-dollar deals for breakfast.

So why was it he couldn't win an argument with his daughter when it came to *eating* breakfast?

"I want pancakes."

Still in her ladybug pajamas, her hair a tangled mess of curls—proof of another battle he'd already lost this morning—Hannah slouched in the dining room chair in a classic pout.

"Hannah…"

The key to winning any negotiation was coming to the table from a place of power, and in this, Jamison had none. Zip. Zilch. Nada. Not after he'd given in to her request for pancakes the day before.

But how was he supposed to stay strong when his daughter's willful tantrum broke down and she'd whispered, "Mommy let me have pancakes," with tears filling her eyes?

And so he'd given in and learned the hard way a sugar rush was not a myth. Hyped up on the sweet stuff, Hannah had talked almost nonstop after leaving the bridal shop—mostly about the very woman Jamison was trying so hard not to think about.

"Rory says I can wear ribbons in my hair.

"Rory says I'll get to carry a basket filled with roses and can throw them like it's raining flowers.

"Rory says…"

But no matter how much his daughter talked, it was Rory's voice Jamison heard. Her smile that flashed through his mind time and again. Her challenge to him to reassure Hannah that everything would be okay and her misplaced confidence that he would succeed.

His daughter didn't need him to encourage her to walk down the aisle and be the best flower girl she could be. Rory had done all that on her own. Jamison doubted there was much the woman couldn't talk a person into if she tried.

Sometimes people let me down.

Whoever the man was—and Jamison would bet the partnership up for grabs that it was a man—he had to be the biggest kind of fool to put that shadow of disappointment in Rory's eyes.

And Jamison was no fool. He learned from his mistakes and the biggest one he'd made was in believing he could make a woman happy. So he'd be smart and keep his distance from the pretty wedding coordinator before she could learn the hard way he could only be another man who would let her down.

Jamison scraped a hand over his face, feeling the stubble he had yet to shave away. He'd grabbed a quick shower that morning, but Hannah had been up by the time he'd gotten dressed. He had hoped she might sleep in, but she awoke first thing…looking as bright eyed and well rested as if she hadn't taken ten years off his life when she woke up screaming in the middle of the night.

His mother-in-law, Louisa, had warned him about deviating from Hannah's schedule. *She's been through so much. She takes comfort in a stable routine.*

In that, they were alike, but lately he'd noticed his daughter's routine—or more specifically, Louisa's routine for his daughter—left very little time for him to spend with Hannah.

After the accident, he'd welcomed his mother-in-law's help. Though not life threatening, Hannah's injuries had left her bruised and broken, and Jamison had almost been afraid to touch her. Louisa, a former nurse, had the knowledge and experience Jamison lacked. But now that Hannah had healed, it was time for Louisa to take a step back—whether she wanted to or not.

Which was one of the reasons he'd insisted on this extended trip with Hannah. He'd thought his mother-in-law had exaggerated the problems he might cause, but now he had to wonder.

The first night at the hotel, bedtime had been accompanied by multiple requests for night-night stories, drinks of water and trips to the bathroom. Had those delay tactics been something more than a child's typical resistance to bedtime in a strange location? Were the nightmares that haunted Hannah enough to make her afraid to close her eyes?

Jamison hated the helplessness that gripped him and how the sound of her cries took him back to that horrible day.

On the phone fighting with Monica, Hannah crying in the background...his wife's shrill scream, the sickening crash of metal and after that...nothing. Just a dead phone clutched in his hand.

Eventually Hannah had drifted off to sleep, her breathing still shaky from lingering tears. But Jamison hadn't slept a wink. Blinking through blurry eyes, he figured he looked every bit as rough as that sleepless night had felt.

He was relieved Hannah didn't seem to be suffering any ill effects, but the sense of anxiety that had kept his eyes wide-open still lingered. The monster under the bed ready to jump out at any minute, even during the day with the sun shining.

"I've already ordered breakfast," he reminded her now as he sank into a chair and was met with her pouty face.

Stick with the routine, he reminded himself.

When he first read through Louisa's list of approved foods, dominated by fruits and vegetables, he'd wondered if his mother-in-law wasn't setting him up for a fall. Really, what kid wanted oatmeal for breakfast? But the pancake incident and last night's nightmare made him realize he didn't need to blame Louisa for his failures.

He could fail spectacularly all on his own.

"But I want—"

A quick knock on the door interrupted the brewing

tantrum, and Jamison wasn't sure when he'd felt more re-lieved. "See, there's room service now with breakfast."

"Pancakes!" Hannah finished in a voice loud enough to have him cringing as he opened the door. And then cring-ing again at who was on the other side.

"Morning!" Looking bright, chipper and far too tempt-ing for so early in the morning, Rory McClaren met his frown with a beaming smile.

Her dark hair was pulled back in a high ponytail that made her look even younger than he guessed she was and brought to mind old sitcoms set back in the '60s. So did the halter-style dress with its soft floral print and full skirt. His mind still foggy from a sleepless night and too many hours spent thinking of her, Jamison could only stare.

After Hannah's nightmare, Rory looked like something out of a dream. As the rich, strong scent of caffeine hit him, he belatedly noticed the silver serving cart in front of her.

"What are you doing here?" Still on some kind of sleep-deprived delay, the question didn't form until Rory had al-ready wheeled the cart between the floral-print couch and coffee table in the living area and into the dining room.

She shot a questioning glance over her bare shoulder. "You did order room service, didn't you?"

Her blue gaze was filled with wide-eyed innocence, but Jamison wasn't buying it. Realizing he was still hold-ing the door open, he let go and followed her inside. "Yes, but I didn't expect the wedding coordinator to deliver it."

She waved a dismissive hand. "Small hotel. Everyone pitches in." Smiling at his daughter, she asked, "Are you ready for breakfast this morning, Miss Hannah?"

Despite her earlier fascination with the woman, Han-nah retreated back into shyness. She drew her bare feet up onto the seat and wrapped her arms around her ladybug-covered legs, looking impossibly tiny in the adult-size chair. "I want pancakes," she repeated, her voice more of a whisper this time.

Instead of a wave of embarrassment crashing over him, Jamison couldn't help feeling a little smug as Rory's cheery expression faltered a bit.

"Um—" she glanced at the ticket tucked beneath one of the covered trays "—it looks like the chef made you oatmeal this morning." She lifted her gaze to Jamison for confirmation.

He nodded. "Oatmeal's good for you. Healthy."

At least that was what his in-laws thought. It wasn't something his mother would have fixed when he was a kid. Not that his mother fixed much of anything in the way of meals—breakfast or otherwise. Jamison had mostly been on his own and, in all honesty, more than content with sugary cereal eaten straight from the box, parked in front of morning cartoons.

"Good for you. Right..." Rory drew out the word as she pulled the cover off the bowl of plain, beige cereal. No fun shapes, bright colors or magically delicious marshmallows there. "What do you say we make this oatmeal even yummier, Hannah?"

Somehow, Jamison should have known a bowl of mush wouldn't be enough to throw her off her game.

"How?" A wealth of doubt filled that one word, and just like that Jamison's amusement vanished.

Yesterday, Hannah had been ready to believe Rory was a fairy godmother who walked on flower petals. And okay, so he didn't buy into Rory McClaren's brand of happily-ever-after, but his daughter was still a little girl. Did he want her doubting something as simple as breakfast couldn't somehow get better?

"I'm guessing Rory has an idea about that," he murmured.

He caught her look of surprise before pleasure brought a pink glow to her cheeks. "That's right. Thanks to your daddy, who also ordered some fruit, we are going to turn this into happy oatmeal."

"Happy?"

"Yep. This oatmeal's a little sad and plain right now," she said as she reached for the platter of fruit beautifully arranged in the middle of the tray. "But with a little bit of color…" Her hands, as delicate and graceful as the rest of her, sliced up the fruit as she spoke. A moment later, she'd outlined a blueberry smiley face in the bowl of oatmeal, complete with banana-slice eyes, a strawberry nose and an orange-wedge smile.

Scrambling up onto her knees, Hannah peered into the bowl Rory set in front of her and let out a soft giggle. "Look, Daddy, the oatmeal's smiling at me."

And his daughter was smiling at him. Jamison would have liked the credit, but Rory McClaren had the magic touch. A woman who thought rainbow was a color and turned plain beige oatmeal into a bright, happy-faced breakfast.

"I like smiley-face yummy oatmeal." Grabbing the spoon, Hannah leaned over the bowl, ready to dig in, her blond hair falling into her face.

"Oops, hold on a second, Hannah."

Skirting around the whitewashed oak table, Rory reached up and pulled the peach-colored band from her ponytail. Jamison's mouth went dry as she gave her head a quick shake and sent her dark hair tumbling over her bare shoulders.

His tongue practically stuck to the roof of his mouth; he fought to swallow, assailed by the image of that silken hair spread out against a pillow or tumbling over *his* shoulders as Rory leaned down to kiss him…

"Thank you, Miss Rory." Her riot of curls contained, Hannah beamed up at the beautiful brunette.

Cupping her chin in one hand, Rory bent down until they were eye to eye. "You are welcome, Miss Hannah."

Hannah giggled at the formality before digging into her breakfast. She bounced up and down in the chair in time with chowing down on a bite of banana, drawing an indulgent smile from Rory.

"And what about you, Mr. Porter?" she asked as she walked back over to the serving tray and waved a hand. "I don't see another bowl of oatmeal for you."

"Coffee," he said abruptly, still trying to get the erotic images out of his mind.

Mistaking the reason for his short response, her earnest gaze met his. "I'm sorry if I overstepped with the ponytail. My only excuse is to say it's an occupational hazard."

"So, wedding coordinator, room service attendant and hairstylist?"

"Oh, I'm not a professional stylist by any means. But in my short time as wedding coordinator, I've learned to be a jack-of-all-trades when it comes to last-minute emergencies. Whether it's figuring out how to turn three bridesmaids' bouquets into four because the bride made up with her best friend at the last second or pulling out a hot-glue gun for a quick repair to a torn hemline, I feel like I've already been there, done that. And now it's like I can't help fixing things… Not that Hannah's broken or you need help and—I have got to learn to keep my mouth shut and my hands to myself!"

Rory wasn't the only one with that second problem, but it wasn't his daughter's hair Jamison longed to get his hands on. "It's all right," he said gruffly, even though it wasn't. Her actions were innocent. His intentions…not so much. "About the ponytail thing, I mean. Anyone can see I can't get it right. And I do mean anyone, since even Hannah tells me her hair looks funny when I'm done with it."

"I'm sure you're doing fine."

"Are you?" The sympathy in her eyes told him he and Hannah had been a topic of conversation once they left the bridal shop. "Because I'm not sure of a damn thing."

He half expected some meaningless platitude, but instead she reached for the carafe on the serving tray and poured a cup of steaming coffee. "Rough night?" she asked as she handed him the mug.

His fingers overlapped hers, the warmth seeping through coming more from her soft skin than from the hard ceramic. For a brief second, they both froze, connected by the fragrant cup of coffee. And he found himself desperate for someone to confide in.

"Nightmare," he admitted as Rory released the mug and took a quick step back. She set about tidying the serving tray, her lashes lowered as she avoided his gaze.

"You or Hannah?"

Jamison gave a quick laugh. "Hannah," he said as if he hadn't had more than his share of bad dreams over the past months. Not about Monica, like the dreams that had Hannah crying out for a mother who would never again kiss away her tears, but ones about the accident.

He'd seen pictures of what remained of the run-down sedan Monica had been driving—a mangled wreck of metal Hannah had somehow survived. As if those images weren't bad enough, his subconscious tormented him even further. In his nightmares, the car burst into flames, plunged into a river or fell from a cliff while he could do nothing but watch.

In reality, Jamison hadn't seen the accident, but he'd heard it.

Worse, he'd caused it.

Chapter Four

"Oh, Ms. McClaren, I have to tell you we just got back from the wedding-cake tasting, and every one of them was to die for. I think all those tiny little bites added up to an entire cake by the time we made up our minds."

Rory smiled as the beaming, sugar-filled bride-to-be rushed to her side in the middle of Hillcrest House's elegant, dark-walnut-paneled lobby. She had offered to take Jamison and Hannah on a tour of the grounds, but so far they hadn't made it out of the hotel. She'd been stopped a handful of times either by guests or employees with questions about upcoming events.

Susannah Erickson was the latest interruption. "I'm glad you enjoyed the tasting. I learned within my first few days here not to accompany brides to the bakery. Too much temptation."

And why, oh, why did she have to say *temptation*? Just speaking the word out loud had her thinking about that

morning, and not about food. The image of Jamison open-
ing the door, dressed but fresh from the shower, was seared
in Rory's mind. The scent of soap and shampoo had clung
to his skin, and his damp hair had been rumpled from a
quick toweling. Add to that the dark stubble he'd yet to
shave away, and all she'd been able to think about was the
seductive rasp of that rough skin against her own…

Almost against her will, Rory sought Jamison out. He
stood off to the right with Hannah at his side, but Rory had
already known that. She'd felt hyperaware of his proxim-
ity since he'd opened the door. Telling herself in the inti-
mate setting of the Bluebell suite, of course she would
notice the overwhelming presence of a masculine, six-
foot-something man.

But even now, surrounded by guests and employees
in the spacious lobby, she was still conscious of him. Of
the way his gray gaze focused on her. Of the way the air
crackled with electricity when their eyes met. Of the restless energy that seemed to pulse inside every inch of his
broad-shouldered frame.

As Rory spoke with the bride-to-be about menu options
and table settings, her words trembled and tripped on her
tongue as though she were the one experiencing a high-
octane sugar rush. Fortunately, her client didn't seem to
pick up on her nerves and promised to call back and book
Hillcrest for her wedding as soon as she had a chance to
talk with her fiancé.

After saying her farewells to Susannah, Rory braced
herself to face Jamison again. He had taken the opportu-
nity to shave and comb his hair during the time it took
for her to return the breakfast dishes and serving cart to
the kitchen. Too bad she didn't find that strong, smooth
jawline and the hint of an expensive, spicy aftershave any
less attractive.

But the clean-cut version was a good reminder of who the man was. In the suite this morning, he'd been a harried father who'd needed her. A man dealing with the heartache of raising a child on his own. A man her heart urged her to help...

This, though, was Jamison Porter, Esquire. A businessman in control of himself and immune to his surroundings as his thumbs flew over his phone. Including, she feared, the daughter twisting restlessly at his side.

Rory knew what it was like to be pushed aside, forgotten, ignored...

She'd been a few years older than Hannah when tragedy struck her family. As an adult, she understood that her parents loved her every bit as much as they loved her brother, Chance, but in the weeks following his accident she'd felt like a ghost wandering the hospital halls—unseen, unheard.

Shaking off the memories, she scolded herself for projecting her own past onto the father and daughter in front of her. *Focus, Rory. Jamison Porter is part of a wedding party and dealing with him part of your job.*

Pasting a professional smile onto her face, she apologized as she joined them. "Sorry about all the interruptions."

"If there's one thing I understand, it's work." He thrust the phone into the pocket of his slacks, but Rory couldn't tell if he was reluctant or relieved to break the connection. "I'm good at what I do."

Rory frowned. The words didn't sound like bragging as much as they sounded like...an apology? She wasn't sure she had that right until his gaze dropped to the top of his daughter's head and his throat worked in a rough swallow.

Suddenly the puzzle pieces fell into place. Successful businessman, not-so-successful family man. His fingers tapped on the outside of his muscular thigh, and Rory could sense his need to reach for his phone again—tangible proof of the predictable, logical world he'd left behind.

"Jamison—"

"I want cake for breakfast," Hannah cut in, her tone grumpy enough for Rory to know the little girl hadn't totally gotten over having to eat oatmeal that morning.

"Only brides get cake for breakfast," her father answered quickly.

"I wanna be a bride."

His daughter's comeback was even faster than his and left Jamison groaning in response. Rory couldn't help but laugh. "Relax, Dad, that's one worry you can put off for a few years." Gazing down at Hannah, she asked, "Do you want to go see where Miss Lindsay is going to get married? You can practice being her flower girl."

Hannah was quiet for a second before her eyes lit up. "Do flower girls get cake?"

"They do—but not for breakfast."

After heaving a sigh at the unfairness of that, Hannah nodded. "Okay."

"All right then. Let's go!"

"Wait, Miss Rory," the girl demanded. "You hafta hold my hand."

Hannah held out her left hand, her right already wrapped around her father's. Rory hesitated even though she knew she was being ridiculous. In her short time at Hillcrest, she'd held more than her share of little and big girls' hands leading up to a wedding. This was nothing different. But with Jamison on the other side, his daughter joining the two of them together, Rory felt a connection that went far beyond a professional capacity.

Something about the corporate lawyer, something in the shadows lingering in his silver eyes, grabbed hold of her. She'd been telling the truth when she said she'd become a jack-of-all-trades with a quick fix for prewedding emergencies. But she had to be careful. She'd be foolish to think she could step in and fix Jamison and his adorable daughter. Foolish to invest too much of herself when their time in Clearville was temporary. Foolish to think he'd want her to.

Though Rory didn't want to be so in tune with the man just a child's length away, she sensed the deep breath he exhaled as they stepped out into the cool morning air. Hannah bounced between them down the wraparound porch's front steps, but it was Jamison who seemed to have released a negative energy bottled up far too long.

As they walked down the gravel path leading from the house, Rory couldn't help glancing back over her shoulder. Even though she'd been back for almost three months, the sight of the Victorian mansion never failed to steal her breath.

She loved the history and old-fashioned elegance of the place. The way it brought to mind a simpler time. With its high peaks, glorious turrets and carved columns and balustrades, an air of romance surrounded the house and property.

Not that romance was anything Rory should be thinking of—at least not as her gaze met Jamison's.

"Um, did you know Hillcrest House was built in the late 1800s? The original owner made his fortune decades earlier down in San Francisco during the gold rush. Not that he ever found gold, but he was one of the enterprising men who figured out the more practical side of gold fever. The thousands of men dreaming of striking it rich were going to need tools and equipment, and he was one of the first on the scene to set up shop."

"Let me guess...at ridiculously inflated rates?" Jamison

asked, the corner of his mouth lifted in a cynical smile that still managed to trip up Rory's heartbeat.

"Oh, but he wasn't just selling metal pans and shovels and pails... He was selling the miners the tools they needed to follow their dreams." Catching the look of utter disbelief on Jamison's face, Rory let out the laughter she'd been holding back. "Yeah, okay, even I can't pull that one off. He robbed the poor suckers blind, selling on credit and then cashing in on their claims when they couldn't pay him back."

"So much for the romance of a time gone by."

Rory started, feeling as if Jamison had read her thoughts moments earlier. "Well, uh, if it's any consolation, karma did bite back, and he ended up losing his fortune—and Hillcrest House—when the stock market crashed."

"Hmm, sounds like cosmic justice but, again, not very romantic."

"Ah, but that's when the house's luck changed. After it stood empty for years, a wealthy industrialist from back east came to California and fell in love with a young woman. He bought Hillcrest as a wedding present for his bride. The story goes that their plan was to have a dozen or so kids—"

"A dozen?"

"At least," Rory emphasized, smiling at the overwhelmed expression on his face as he glanced down at his lone child. "Sadly, they were unable to have children, but as time went on and more and more people were traveling to California and taking vacations along the coast, they decided to turn Hillcrest into a hotel so its rooms could still be filled with families and children and laughter—even if those families only stayed for a short time."

The reminder was one Rory needed to focus on. Jamison and Hannah were only staying for a few weeks.

She couldn't allow herself to be drawn in on a personal level, to let herself start to care too much, too quickly. But with the little girl's hand tucked so trustingly in hers as she sang under her breath, Rory couldn't help wondering if it was already too late.

Hannah's shy sweetness reminded Rory of a kitten she'd once rescued. The frightened Siamese had been all eyes in a skinny body covered with matted fur. It had taken time to build up enough trust for the kitten to allow her to pet it and even more time for the tiny bundle of fur to completely come out of its shell. To learn to run and play and chase. But Rory hadn't given up, because even at the beginning, underneath all the wariness, she had sensed the playful kitten longing to come out.

And as much as the kitten had needed to be rescued, Rory had needed something to save. She couldn't compare her experience as a child to what Hannah was facing in losing her mother so young, but Rory understood a little of what the girl was going through.

That beneath the sadness and loss, a silly, playful girl was struggling to break free.

"And what's your family's connection to the hotel?"

The summer breeze blew a lock of chestnut hair across Jamison's forehead and let loose a flurry of butterflies in her stomach. He was so good-looking, she forgot the question, forgot everything as she met his gaze over his daughter's head.

"Rory."

Heat flooded her cheeks as she tore her attention from the heat shimmering between them and back on what should have been her focus all along. "Right...my family's connection to the hotel. Um, the couple owned the hotel for decades, but with no children to leave it to, they put it up for sale. My grandparents met at Hillcrest—"

"Another romantic story?"

"Exactly," she answered, pleased with his guess despite the cynical tone of the question. "My grandmother was working the front desk and my grandfather was a guest here. Years later, when they heard the hotel was available, they bought it as an investment. They visited all the time but never lived here.

"My father and my uncle both worked here when they were younger, but the hotel and the hospitality industry were never their calling. Not like it was for my aunt Evelyn. Everyone knew she would run Hillcrest one day. She's smart and strong and independent."

Rory's worry over her aunt's health stung her eyes, but she blinked, banishing the tears before they could form. Her aunt wouldn't appreciate Rory getting teary in front of a guest. Not even if that guest was ridiculously handsome with the kind of broad shoulders and strong arms where a woman would be tempted to find comfort.

"And you and your cousin are here helping out?"

That was the explanation she and Evie had been giving people. Their aunt kept a strict line drawn between her personal and professional life, and she didn't want anyone outside of family to know of her health problems.

"Hillcrest House has always been a popular location for weddings with the locals in Clearville and Redfield," Rory said, naming another nearby town, "but last year my aunt decided to expand Hillcrest as a wedding destination. The couples now have the choice of an all-inclusive ceremony, with the hotel handling everything from the cake to the music to the photographer."

"And that's where you come in."

"I work with the couple to get a feel of the type of wedding they're looking for and design all the elements to match that theme."

Jamison shook his head at the notion of a wedding theme, which had Rory wondering what his wedding to Hannah's mother had been like. Not that she was about to ask.

"You're good at this."

Feeling her cheeks heat at the surprising compliment, Rory shook her head. "I've had Hillcrest House facts drilled into my head since I was a little girl. I could recite this information in my sleep. A couple of times, in the midst of wedding madness, I think maybe I have!"

"Not just the tour. I mean the way you dealt with the guests and the staff earlier. You're friendly and encouraging but firm enough to get your point across."

"I—thank you," Rory said, far more pleased by the compliment than she should have been. She didn't like thinking of herself as hungry for approval, but after her failure at the interior design firm in LA, finding success—especially at Hillcrest House—was so important to her. "I didn't expect…"

"Expect what?"

She gave a small laugh. "You and my cousin Evie have quite a bit in common when it comes to the whole wedding thing."

Jamison and her by-the-book cousin likely had more in common than their negative views on weddings and marriage. A CPA, Evie was smart, well educated, as razor sharp as the blunt cut of her dark, chin-length hair. She was practical, pragmatic and more than a little cynical—the kind of woman Rory figured would impress a successful businessman like Jamison.

Ignoring the stab of jealousy at the thought of Jamison and her cousin forming their own mutual-admiration society, Rory said, "Evie's a genius when it comes to handling the books and the last person to believe in fairy tales, but sometimes she acts like I pull off these weddings with nothing more than a wave of a magic wand. She doesn't seem to notice the hard work that goes into them."

"Look, Daddy!" Hannah's impatient tug on their hands brought the conversation to a halt as they reached a curve in the pathway. An intricate lattice-arched entry led to the rose garden—a favorite spot for many brides and grooms to say their vows. Pink, red and white blooms unfurled amid the dark green bushes and the thick, rich lawn.

Turning to Rory, Hannah asked, "Is that where you grow the flowers for the flower girls?"

Not about to ruin the moment for the child, especially when she saw some of that curiosity shining through in her big brown eyes, Rory said, "It sure is. Why don't you go look for the perfect flower? But don't touch, okay? Some of the roses have sharp thorns."

Hannah's pale brows furrowed as she glanced between the rose garden and back again. "Will you stay right here, Daddy?"

"I'm not going anywhere, Hannah Banana."

A small smile tugged at the little girl's lips, and Rory swore the sweet expression was somehow tied to the strings around her heart. She couldn't help smiling as Hannah tucked her hands behind her back before racing—somewhat awkwardly—over to the garden.

But it was Jamison and the unabashed tenderness in his eyes as he gazed at his daughter that had Rory's emotions all tangled up in knots.

He was a guest. And like any other guest who passed through Hillcrest House, Rory would quickly forget all about him. She'd forget all about this day, about walking with Jamison and Hannah beneath a cloudless sky. About the warmth of his skin as his arm brushed against hers. About the rich, masculine scent that tempted her to move closer and breathe deeper. About the longing to reach out and take his hand, knowing how something as simple as entwining her fingers with his would form a bond she would feel right down to her bones...

Yes, indeed, she would forget all about that. Might just spend the rest of her life forgetting all about that.

The strict talking-to had Rory straightening her shoulders and adopting a polite smile, neither of which were any protection against the power behind Jamison's gaze.

"I'll say it again, Rory. You're good at what you do," he repeated, the intensity behind his words preempting any denial she might have made. "Anyone who doesn't appreciate you is a fool."

"Like this, Miss Rory?" Hannah asked over her shoulder as she placed a single rose petal on the verdant green grass.

"Just like that!"

Jamison shook his head at the beautiful brunette's unrelenting encouragement. "You do realize, at that rate, it'll take her an hour and a half to walk down the aisle?"

"She is the flower girl, and they are her flowers. She has every reason to enjoy her moment."

How was it that Rory McClaren seemed to enjoy every moment? A hint of pink touched her cheeks, and he couldn't help wondering if it was from the midmorning sun—or in response to the words he shouldn't have spoken.

Mouth shut and hands to yourself, Porter, he repeated, glad he'd at least stuck to the second part of the mantra despite the serious temptation she posed at every turn. His finger itched to discover the softness of the dark hair that trailed down her back, to trace the splash of freckles across the elegant line of her collarbones, to strip away the strap of her dress marring the perfection of her shoulder...

He hadn't touched, but he couldn't seem to stop himself from speaking. He'd seen the self-consciousness she tried to hide as she talked about her aunt and cousin—smart, successful women—as if she were something less. And everything in him had rebelled at hearing it.

Yes, Rory was beautiful, but desire was something he could control. Listening to her put herself down, even if the words had been unspoken, that was something he couldn't let go. Not after all she'd done for Hannah in as little as two days.

And yeah, it scared the hell out of him, when at times his daughter still felt like a stranger to him. When he felt at such a loss for what to do or what to say. When he felt himself start to shut down like he had when he was a kid and his parents' fighting was enough to send him underneath the covers—or sometimes even underneath the bed—where he'd cover his ears and close his eyes and wish himself away.

But right now, in this moment with Hannah jumping from one spot to the next, playing some kind of flower-petal hopscotch, he wouldn't have wished himself anywhere else in the world.

"Thank you."

Rory blinked in surprise. "For what?"

"For Hannah. I haven't seen her this happy in—I'm not sure I remember when."

She shook her head. "It's not me. It's Hillcrest. This place is magical that way."

When Jamison offered a disbelieving snort in response, she held up a silencing hand. "Hear me out." And when that hand came down and she entwined her fingers with his, he couldn't have said a word anyway.

Holding hands hadn't made it into his fantasy, but it might have if he'd known how something so simple would make his pulse skyrocket, his heart race, his stomach muscles tighten in response. The softness of her skin seemed to telegraph through his entire body until he swore he could feel her caress...everywhere.

He wasn't sure how he got his feet to move as she led him over toward a white wrought iron bench. Tucked off to the side of the garden, the shaded spot offered a perfect view of Hannah playing a few yards away.

"Rory—" His voice was a strangled croak, and even when she let go, the feel of her hand gliding away branded him. It was all he could do not to scrub his palm against his pressed khakis.

She patted the spot beside her. "Have a seat. Please," she added when he stood ramrod straight at her side.

Somehow, he made his muscles move and forced himself to sit on a bench too small for the arm's-length distance he needed between them. So small the cool breeze carried the sunshine-and-wildflower scent of her skin closer and a strand of her hair danced over his biceps like a caress.

It took everything in his power to focus on the words she was saying rather than following the tantalizing movement of her lips, but the seriousness in her blue eyes soon caught his complete attention. "I have an older brother, Chance, who I adore. He's four years older than I am, and growing up he was always my hero. The big brother who looked out for me. When I was a few years older than Hannah, he was in an accident."

Even though years had passed, Rory sucked in a deep breath before telling the next part. "He was showing off for his friends, fell off his skateboard doing some crazy jump and hit his head. He ended up in a coma. The doctors did everything they could, but for a long time, they didn't know if he would wake up or what kind of shape he would be in if he did."

"I can imagine how hard that must have been on you and your parents." Hannah's injuries hadn't been that severe, but it was the months leading up to the accident when he hadn't known if he would ever see his daughter again and the agonizing hours after that final fight with Monica when he hadn't even known if Hannah was still *alive* that gave him an idea of what the McClarens had gone through.

"It was. Our family had always been so together, so strong, but Chance's accident proved how everything could change. Like that," she said with a snap of her fingers. "As the weeks went by, and his condition didn't change, eventually my dad went back to work. Not because his job was more important than Chance, but because—I just don't think he could sit there, feeling so hopeless, anymore.

"My mom refused to leave my brother's side—eating, sleeping, living at the hospital. She never came out and said so, at least not when I was around, but I think she resented my dad for not doing the same."

"And what did you do," Jamison asked, "during all that time?"

Rory met his gaze before ducking her head, looking almost embarrassed that he'd asked about her. He could imagine she must have felt like the forgotten child, the healthy, happy one no one had the time or energy to pay much attention to.

"I split my days between school and the hospital. I mostly tried to be quiet and stay out of the way, but as the weeks went on... I don't know, maybe I got to be more like my dad, where I couldn't sit there and watch anymore. And then one day, after my mom had run down to the cafeteria for coffee, she came back and I was kneeling on the bed, shaking Chance and shouting at him to stop messing around and to wake up."

"Rory."

Shaking off his sympathy, she talked faster, as if eager to get through the worst of it. "After that…incident, my aunt and uncle, Evie's parents, brought the two of us here for an extended vacation. We ran and laughed and played and explored every inch of this place.

"Not that I forgot about Chance. Every game of pretend Evie and I played over the summer had something to do with breaking a curse or casting a spell or rescuing him from a dragon. I knew if I believed strongly enough, one day Chance would open his eyes and wake up… And one day, he did."

"I'm glad your brother got better, and I can see why, as a little girl, this place would seem so magical, but Rory—" Jamison stopped short and heaved out a heavy sigh. "Hannah's mother isn't going to open her eyes and wake up. Not for all the faith or magic or fairy tales in the world."

"No, she isn't. And Hannah's been through a horrible tragedy, but she's still a little girl who wants to run and laugh and play again, and she needs to know it's okay for her to do those things."

"Of course it's okay."

"And she knows this…how? By watching you? When was the last time you ran or laughed or just enjoyed life a little?"

"Give me a break, Rory. I'm a grown man, not a kid."

"Right. But you're a grown man *with* a kid. A child who's lost her mother. She's looking to you to see how she's supposed to react to a loss she isn't old enough to understand."

Jamison jerked away from Rory's imploring gaze to focus on Hannah. She was no longer dropping petals but was instead gathering them up, one by one. Picking up the pieces…

He didn't want to admit Rory was right, but the truth

was he'd spent his entire life burying his feelings. Was it any wonder he'd done the same when Monica died?

But he hadn't thought about how his emotions—or his lack of emotion—were affecting Hannah. He'd seen how she had retreated into herself after the accident, so different from the smiling, laughing girl he remembered.

How had he not seen his own reflection staring back at him when he looked at his daughter?

"Even before...Monica," he confessed, "I wasn't the running and laughing kind of guy."

A small smile played around Rory's lips, telling him she wasn't shocked by his confession. "And that's why I wanted you to come along today. So you could see that here, at Hillcrest House, you can be."

"Wait a minute." Jamison reared back against the wrought iron bench and waved a hand in the direction of the path they'd taken. "You're telling me this whole tour was for my sake and not for Hannah's?" It was by far the most ridiculous—and quite possibly the sweetest—thing anyone had ever done for him.

"Hillcrest House is special that way," she told him. "Its magic seems to touch whoever needs it the most."

Somehow his scoffing laugh stuck in his throat. There was no magic, and hadn't he already decided there couldn't be any touching? He wasn't the kind of romantic fool who would buy into such whimsical nonsense.

But in the peaceful setting with the dappled sunlight streaming through the trees and the gentle understanding reflected in Rory's midnight blue eyes, Jamison almost wished that he was.

Chapter Five

Jamison Porter had to think she was the world's biggest fool. Had she really spent the past five minutes trying to convince a corporate lawyer, a man who lived his life based on rules and regulations, to believe in magic?

No wonder he was staring at her. The poor man was probably trying to figure out a way to grab his child and run before the crazy lady totally fell off her rocker. She would have been more embarrassed—probably *should* have been more embarrassed—except she believed every word she said. Hillcrest *was* magical, the kind of place to bring people together, and if he gave it half a chance, Jamison might feel that, too.

A tug on her skirt broke the moment, freeing her from that intense silver stare, as she turned to Hannah.

"Miss Rory?" The little girl ducked her head shyly as she pointed to a glimpse of white showing between the trees in the distance. "What's that?"

"That, Miss Hannah, is my favorite spot in the world."

"Your favorite spot in the whole, whole world?"

After pressing her knuckles to her chin and pretending to think for a moment, Rory nodded. "The whole, whole world."

Hannah offered a lightning-quick smile, one Rory couldn't help returning. Playing to the child's curiosity, she stood and held out her hand. "Do you want to go see?"

After hesitating for a moment, Hannah asked, "Can Daddy come, too?"

Without looking his way, she offered, "I bet your daddy would love to come with us."

Jamison made a sound Rory decided to take as an agreement as she led the way down the flagstone path. "What about you, Hannah?" she asked the little girl. "Do you have a favorite place?"

The little girl gave a soft giggle. "The hidey-hole in Daddy's office."

Rory laughed. "A hidey-hole, Jamison? I mean, I've been known to duck behind an ice sculpture to avoid a bridezilla or two, but I've never had to install a hidey-hole."

"It's not a hole, it's—" He shook his head. "Your favorite spot, Hannah? Really?" he asked, surprise softening his expression.

His daughter nodded as she swung the two adults' arms back and forth in time with her steps. "Yep. It's just my size an' when I'm real quiet, nobody knows I'm there. Like the time I hid from Nana."

"Yes, well, your grandmother isn't as good at hide-and-seek as you are," Jamison said, his wry tone telling Rory the older woman hadn't been as amused with her granddaughter's game as Hannah was, either. With a glance at Rory, he said, "And it's not a hole. The furniture set in my home office came with a liquor cabinet. I'm more a beer-on-the-weekend than a three-martini-lunch kind of guy, so I never bothered to stock the cabinet. Probably a good thing, since someone—" he gently shook Hannah's arm "—thinks it's a fun place to hide."

Jamison thought he was struggling as a father, but he must be doing something right. Didn't he realize Hannah's favorite place was one she associated with him?

As they rounded a bend along the flagstone pathway, Rory announced, "And here it is. My favorite place in the whole, whole world."

Rory was accustomed to breathless reactions at this point, and Hannah did not disappoint. "Daddy, look! It's a playhouse."

"I see it, Hannah," Jamison answered, and Rory couldn't help wondering *what* he saw.

With its crisscross latticework, carved pillars and wide steps leading toward the circular platform, the gazebo was breathtaking. The gleaming white woodwork could be transformed by wrapping the columns with gorgeous flowered garlands, adding colorful organza swags to the decorative eaves or bunting to the airy facade.

It was one of the most romantic spots Rory could imagine, and she'd shown it to dozens of couples in her short time as Hillcrest's wedding coordinator. But showing it to Jamison felt...different.

She felt oddly vulnerable, as if she were revealing a part of herself to the enigmatic, troubling man at her side.

Needing to create some distance, she let go of Hannah's hand and tried to pretend this was no different from any other tour. "It does look like a playhouse, but it's a gazebo, and this is where Lindsay is getting married." Pointing to the wide steps, she added, "Ryder and your daddy will be standing right up there, waiting. Because you're the flower girl, you'll go first—"

"An' get to throw my flowers."

"You'll throw your flowers and Robbie will carry the rings. Lindsay's bridesmaids will walk down the aisle and finally Lindsay."

"'Cause she's the bride and gets to eat cake for breakfast," the little girl piped with a definitive nod.

"That's right, and she'll walk right up here and—" Rory had barely set foot on the first step when she heard a creak and a crack. Neither sound registered until the board splintered beneath her sandal and pain shot up her leg. Her abbreviated cry got stuck in her throat as she lost her balance and fell—

Not to the solid ground but against Jamison's solid chest as he caught her in his arms. For a stunned moment, neither of them moved.

"You okay?" His low murmur stirred the hair at her temples and the vibration set off tiny shock waves in her belly.

Staring breathlessly up into his silver eyes, Rory could do little more than nod. Her heart pounded, and she wished she could blame the reaction on her near fall. Instead, she was pretty sure it had everything to do with the man who'd caught her. She braced a hand against his chest, knowing she should move, but her body refused to listen to her brain. The soft cotton was warmed by the morning sun and held the scent of soap combined with 100 percent pure male.

His face was inches from hers, so close she could feel the kiss of his breath against her lips, a prelude to the touch of his mouth against her own…

"Miss Rory!" Hannah's startled cry broke the moment so quickly Rory wasn't sure she hadn't imagined it.

"Stay back, Hannah. It's not safe," Jamison instructed. Bending down, he carefully maneuvered Rory's foot from between the jagged, cracked boards. She winced at the raw scrape on the outside of her ankle.

"She's all bleedy."

The wobble of tears shook Hannah's voice, and Rory focused on the little girl instead of the throbbing pain. "Hey, Hannah, do you—do you know what would make me feel better? If you'd sing a song. Can you do that for me?"

Nodding her head with a big sniff, she started singing a song Rory had heard her humming under her breath on their walk. She wasn't sure which was the bigger distraction— Hannah's sweet voice or the feel of Jamison's hands against her bare skin. She swallowed hard at the sight of the gorgeous man kneeling at her feet and swayed slightly.

Jamison caught her around the waist and lowered her to the first step. "Here, have a seat while I take a look at your ankle."

"Thank you. I—I don't know what happened."

"I can tell you that. The wood's nearly rotted through."

She shook her head. "No, that can't be. Earl, our handyman, just finished remodeling the gazebo last week." She had noticed some wear and tear and had put the gazebo on the handyman's to-do list.

"I'd say all your handyman did was slap on a coat of white paint. Judging by the way that step cracked beneath your feet, that new layer of latex is about all that's holding this thing together."

Dismayed, Rory struggled to push to her feet, but Jamison held her in place. "But this is where Ryder and Lindsay are getting married. It's where I—"

Where *Rory* wanted to get married. Okay, she wasn't even dating anyone and her last relationship had ended in disaster, but none of that meant she'd given up hope of finding true love. She wanted love, marriage, a family... and it all started here. She'd imagined dozens of scenarios for her perfect dream wedding, and while the dress, the flowers, even the guy had changed numerous times, the one constant had been speaking her vows beneath the lacy, romantic gazebo.

"Hey, it's going to be okay." Jamison's voice cut into her thoughts, and only as she met his silver gaze did Rory realize how close he was sitting.

He'd taken the step below her and slipped the sandal from her foot. He cradled her instep in one large hand while he brushed sharp slivers of wood from her abraded skin. The warmth of his body seeped into hers, radiating out from his palm, and Rory shivered in response. She caught the scent of his aftershave again, mixing with the pine-scented breeze surrounding them.

She drew a quick breath in through her mouth, trying to somehow stop inhaling the heady combination, but that only made matters worse as Jamison focused on her parted lips. Her pulse pounded and it was all Rory could do not to lean closer, to close the narrow gap between them, to press her mouth against the temptation of his.

The wind shifted again, rustling through the trees and carrying the sound of Hannah's sweet voice as she started singing a new song...

Jamison reared back, a look akin to horror flashing across his features so quickly, Rory wasn't sure what she had seen. But just like that, it was as though the tender moment never happened.

"You're lucky it wasn't a guest nearly breaking an ankle on that step," he was saying. "This whole thing is a lawsuit waiting to happen. You need signs and a barricade cordoning off the area until someone can tear—"

"Tear it down?" She stared at him as she jerked her foot away. Instantly, the warmth of his touch disappeared, and the throbbing in her ankle multiplied. Was this the same man who'd come to her rescue, catching her when she would have fallen? The same man who'd cradled her foot in those big, warm hands? The same man she'd thought was going to kiss her?

With his arms crossed over his broad chest, *he* might as well have had signs and barricades warning her off.

"I am not letting anyone tear down the gazebo!" She'd as soon rip her own heart out and douse all her dreams of finding true love. Without the gazebo—

He reached out and gave the wobbly railing a good shake. "You won't have to let anyone tear it down. A stiff breeze, and the whole thing will fall over."

Still feeling foolish over the almost kiss she was starting to think had only happened in her own head, she glared at him. "You'd like that, wouldn't you? After all, you've made it clear how you feel about this *whole wedding thing.* You'd probably just as soon tear it down yourself."

"You're being ridiculous," Jamison muttered, but the baleful look he cast at the gazebo told Rory he was considering doing some damage to the structure—with his bare hands.

Pain shot up her leg the instant she pushed to her feet, and Jamison shot her a frustrated look. "Would you sit back down? You're lucky you didn't break your neck, thanks to your beloved gazebo, and you should go to the hospital—"

"No, Daddy!"

Jamison started at his daughter's shout. "Hannah, what?"

The little girl rushed over, but instead of latching onto her father, she threw her arms around Rory's legs, almost knocking her off balance.

Jamison frowned as Rory flinched. "Hannah."

"Don't make Rory go to the hospital! Don't make her go! Mommy went to the hospital and she never, never came back!"

* * *

Jamison froze at his daughter's cry, the sound piercing straight through his heart. In those first dark days after the accident, he'd tried to be there for Hannah, to be the one to care for her, to hold her when she cried. But her tears had been for her mother, and Jamison's fumbling, painful attempts to explain that Monica was now in heaven didn't seem to penetrate Hannah's sorrow.

"No! I want Mommy!" Accusation had filled her dark eyes, as if Jamison was the one keeping Monica away, the one responsible…and in so many ways, he was.

He'd seen the sympathy of the doctors and nurses at the hospital. *Give her time*, they'd advised. *She'll come around.* Before long, he'd learned to step back, to let someone better prepared handle Hannah when she was upset. One step, and then another and another, and before long, he'd stood on the fringes of his daughter's life. Present but accounting for nothing.

"Hannah." He could barely get the word out, barely make himself move to brush a hand against her curls. Half afraid to touch her and 100 percent certain she'd pull away.

Rory had no such fear. "Oh, Hannah, sweetie." Despite her injured ankle, she dropped down to his daughter's level to give her a hug. "I'm fine! All I need is a Band-Aid or two."

She brushed away Hannah's tears, reassuring the little girl who managed a watery smile in response, her ease with his daughter making Jamison feel like even more of a failure as a father.

"See, Daddy? Miss Rory doesn't need to go to the hospital." Hannah stared up at him, her chin set at a stubborn angle.

Jamison fought back a sigh. How did he end up the bad guy in all of this when he was only trying to help? "Hannah…"

"Your daddy was worried about me. And even if I did have to go to the hospital, I promise you I would come back."

He caught sight of the wince she tried to hide as she pushed to her feet and warned, "You need to get some ice on that ankle to keep the swelling down."

"I'll be fine," she repeated with a big smile, and Jamison couldn't figure out if it was for his benefit, his daughter's or her own.

At her first awkward step, he sighed again, wrapped an arm around her waist and under her knees and lifted her against her chest. Her startled gasp brought them face-to-face. Close enough for him to count the freckles dusting her cheeks. Close enough to feel her breath against his skin. And Jamison wondered how long he could have resisted before pulling Rory into his arms—banged-up ankle or no banged-up ankle.

"I'm not letting you hobble all the way back to the hotel."

"Well, you can't carry me back!"

He gave her a light toss, fighting a grin at the way her arms tightened around his neck. "I'm pretty sure I can."

"Not into the hotel. I can't—please, Jamison."

His smile faded. Rory was more than simply flustered by the idea. Pained embarrassment etched her pretty features. He didn't know the reason for the lack of confidence he'd sensed earlier, but he could understand why she wouldn't want her coworkers to see a guest carrying her through the hotel—regardless of the situation. Still, he couldn't let her limp back on her own. "Rory…"

"You, um… My place isn't far from here."

"Your place? You don't have a room at the hotel?"

She shook her head. "Evie does. She's staying in my aunt's room while she's…away. But I wanted a place of my own. I thought it would be easier."

"Easier?" he asked.

He did his damnedest to ignore the dizzying thought of taking Rory back to her place, but that was as impossible as ignoring the feel of her in his arms as she gave him directions to something called the caretaker's cottage.

She's injured, you idiot, he warned himself. *And your daughter is right beside you.*

Hannah skipped along the path, carrying the shoe he'd slipped from Rory's foot and still humming the song she'd switched to earlier. A song Monica used to sing to her.

It might not have been his dead wife's voice calling out from the grave, but it had still chilled him to the bone.

"I thought it would be easier keeping my professional and personal lives separate," Rory was saying, "if I wasn't staying at the hotel." She didn't meet his gaze, but judging by the color in her cheeks, she was well aware whatever was happening between them was a serious mixing of the two.

She wasn't simply the wedding coordinator any more than he was just the best man.

The best man... He wasn't anywhere near the best man for a woman like Rory. He needed to keep his distance, so how the hell had he ended up with her in his arms, about to carry her into her home?

"Yeah, how's that working out for you?"

She lifted her chin, but the stubborn angle only emphasized the pulse pounding at the base of her neck. "Just fine," she insisted, but as he rounded a curve on the path and the small cottage came into view, he thought he heard her whisper under her breath. "Until now."

Rory had always loved the caretaker's cottage, as the place was still known even though many years had passed since Hillcrest had live-in staff. From what her aunt had told her, the tiny wood-and-stone structure had nearly fallen into disrepair, but decades ago, Evelyn had saved it from the brink of destruction and had kept it up over the years.

Still, it had needed some sprucing up and some serious elbow grease to turn it into a place Rory called home, but now it was her sanctuary. A place she could retreat to where she didn't have to deal with demanding brides, cold-footed grooms or the mess she'd left behind in LA.

As Jamison set her down on the tiny porch, she insisted, "I'll be fine from here."

He'd said little on the walk from the gazebo, but Rory had felt the rock-hard tension gripping his muscles—a tightness she doubted had anything to do with carrying her weight.

She'd practically thrown herself at him thanks to the broken step, and he probably had whiplash from pulling away from her so fast.

"There are still splinters stuck in your ankle. If you won't let me take you—you know where—you're going to need some help."

She felt the weight of his frown as she hop-stepped over to the door and slipped the key out from beneath a brightly colored mosaic pot of pansies. She held her palm out in the universal stop sign as he moved closer. "I'm good. I've got it."

The very, very last thing she needed was Jamison Porter carrying her over the threshold!

"I like your house, Miss Rory," Hannah announced before bending down to take an exaggerated sniff of the pansies.

"Thank you, Miss Hannah."

"She probably thinks seven dwarves live here," Jamison muttered under his breath as Rory pushed the door open.

She shot him a look over her shoulder, though she had

to admit the tiny cottage in the woods did have a fairy-tale feel. The front door opened into the living room, a comfortable space Rory had filled with secondhand finds from the Hope Chest, an eclectic consignment store in town. Two floral-print sofas faced a steamer-trunk coffee table, all in pastel shades with white accents. Hannah was drawn to the patchwork bear sitting in a miniature white wicker rocking chair in the corner, both mementos from Rory's childhood.

"I have a first-aid kit in the bathroom." Rory waved a hand toward the partially open door down the narrow hallway.

"I'll get it. You sit."

Rory flopped onto the sofa with a huff. Sit? What was she, a dog? But as she reached down to massage the bruise already forming on her ankle, she had to admit it felt good to take her weight off. A clatter sounded in the bathroom—something falling into the porcelain sink—followed by Jamison's curse.

"Everything okay in there?"

"Fine. I dropped the—never mind."

Groaning, Rory dropped her head back on the back of the couch as she tried to remember what else she kept in the medicine cabinet along with the Band-Aids and iodine. Just what she wanted—a superhot guy getting a peek at her anti-aging wrinkle cream, Midol and other assorted feminine products.

He returned a moment later, first-aid kit in hand, and while Rory couldn't be sure, she thought his face was a shade or two more red than when he'd entered.

Great.

"Find everything?"

"Uh, yeah. I think so."

And then Rory wasn't so worried about Jamison's embarrassment or even her own as he knelt down in front of her and placed her foot on his khaki-covered thigh. She could feel the muscles and heat beneath her foot and it was all she could do not to flex her toes like some kind of attention-seeking kitten. And while Jamison might have made reference to Snow White, Rory couldn't help feeling a little like Cinderella as he cradled her foot in his large hands.

"How's that?" he asked.

A perfect fit...

Rory snapped herself back to reality as she realized he'd already removed the last of the splinters with a pair of tweezers, dabbed some antibiotic ointment on the scrape and was getting ready to smooth a Band-Aid over the area.

"Good. Fine. Thank you."

His nod sent a lock of hair falling over his forehead, and she gripped the cushions at her side to keep from reaching out. Jamison glanced up and their gazes locked, and Rory knew.

"I'm not imagining things."

His forehead wrinkled in a frown. "I wouldn't think so. I've never heard of a twisted ankle causing hallucinations."

"You were thinking of kissing me earlier."

This time it was Jamison's turn to look like he'd taken a blow to the head. He sucked in a breath that fanned the flames burning in his quicksilver eyes. "Rory. That's not—" His gaze shot to Hannah, who was sitting in the rocking chair, her attention still captured by her newfound stuffed friend. "We can't."

Maybe Rory should have been more disappointed as he turned his attention to cleaning up the cotton balls and wrapping from the first aid, but instead a tiny kernel of hope bloomed in her chest.

Because *can't* was a different story than *didn't want to*.

Chapter Six

"What do you mean, you fired Earl?" Her head pounding almost as loudly as her ankle, Rory stared in disbelief across the wide expanse of her cousin's cherrywood desk. She'd spent a painful half an hour searching for the handyman before stopping by her cousin's office, where Evie had stunned her with the news that she'd let the man go.

"Is that—" Evie frowned as Rory hobbled over to a chair and reached down to rub her ankle. "Why on earth is there toilet paper wrapped around your foot? And why are you limping?"

Rory straightened, heat rising to her cheeks. "Never mind."

Before Jamison and Hannah left the cottage, the little girl had ducked into the bathroom and returned with a long length of the paper trailing behind her. Her blond brows had pulled together in concentration as she'd tried to wrap the "bandage" around Rory's ankle before her father stepped in.

The last thing she'd expected was for Jamison to indulge his daughter's attempts to play doctor, but he'd showed the same seriousness using the toilet paper as when he'd applied the antibacterial ointment and Band-Aids.

Yes, she should have ripped the silly "bandage" off already, but she'd been touched by Hannah's sweetness. Not to mention Jamison's...

"How could you fire Earl without telling me?"

"We agreed when we both started working here that staffing decisions fall under my purview." Evie gazed back at her, slender hands folded in front of her. Sometimes her cousin's crystal-cool demeanor was enough to make Rory want to scream. It made her want *Evie* to scream, to show some emotion, to go back to being the warm, funny girl Rory remembered instead of the calculating woman she'd become.

"Earl wasn't a handyman you can replace with a snap of your fingers." The potbellied, fiftysomething man had worked for the hotel almost as long as Rory could remember. "He was—"

"He was stealing from the hotel," her cousin cut in.

Rory's jaw dropped. "Stealing?" she choked, the word lodging against the lump in her throat.

Pamela Worthington's voice whipped through her mind so clearly, she half expected her former employer to be looming behind her, anger and disappointment written across her aristocratic features. *I trusted you, Aurora. I gave you a chance despite your limited experience, and this is how you repay me? By stealing from our clients?*

"Are you—" Rory cleared her throat before her words could break into ragged shards. "Are you sure? Maybe there was some kind of mistake—"

But Evie was already shaking her head. "He turned in an invoice from Hendrix Hardware a few weeks ago." She tucked a strand of perfectly straight dark hair behind her ear. "Not long after that, I ran into Howard Hendrix, who told me he was sorry the parts Earl special ordered for the new irrigation system didn't work out and if we needed him to order more, to let him know."

"Maybe the parts didn't work. Maybe he bought them somewhere else."

"Where? And why wouldn't Earl have a copy of that receipt? You know Hendrix gives us a better deal than the big-box store over in Redfield. No, Earl returned those parts and pocketed the money."

"But I saw him working on the irrigation."

"And for all we know, he patched everything together with duct tape and used chewing gum. I already have a call in to a landscaping company. Which means spending even more money."

Focusing on the money side of her job was not Rory's strong suit, but Evie had been clear on how tightly the two were tied together.

I know you like picturing yourself as some kind of fairy godmother, but you can't solve things with a wave of a wand. Aunt Evelyn wants to expand the wedding destination aspect of the hotel, but doing so only makes sense if it makes money.

Her cousin had also told her about an offer on the hotel. Their aunt Evelyn had fielded offers from large hotel chains before, but with her recent health issues, Rory feared she might be considering it. Selling Hillcrest...

Rory couldn't even imagine not having the hotel in her family.

"I spoke with Susannah Erickson this morning. She's almost committed to having the ceremony here," Rory told her cousin. "I'll give her a call this afternoon. If I can get them to sign off on the paperwork, I can request a deposit—"

"Rory," Evie said slowly.

Just the sound of her cousin's voice had her stomach sinking. "What is it? What's wrong?"

"As Earl was leaving, he said something under his breath."

Rory frown in confusion. "You just fired him, Evie." She held up a hand as her cousin opened her mouth to protest. "Rightfully so, but I'm sure he had a whole bunch of things to say."

"It wasn't about his being fired, at least not exactly."

"What did he say?"

Evie dropped her gaze to her hands, her inability to make eye contact making that sick feeling in the pit of Rory's stomach even worse. "He said that if his last name was McClaren, he wouldn't be getting fired. He'd be getting promoted to wedding coordinator."

Rory sucked in a quick breath that fanned the flames of humiliation rising in her cheeks. "How—how could he know? How could anyone here know?"

Silence had been a stipulation in keeping the Worthingtons from going to the police. The last thing they wanted was for their clients to know one of their employees had stolen from the multimillion-dollar homes they were hired to stage.

Somehow, though, word had gotten out. And the Worthingtons quickly pointed the finger at Rory—the designer they had fired after finding pictures of the stolen items posted to online auctions from her computer.

She'd not only lost her job, but her career, her friends, her boyfriend, as Peter had taken his mother's side. Only later, once the hurt and humiliation started to wane, had Rory realized why he'd turned on her so easily…

"I don't know, Rory," Evie said, pulling her from the dark memories and how badly things had ended in LA. "I certainly haven't said anything."

A touch of self-righteousness underlined her cousin's words. Of course, Evie wouldn't say anything. Evie would never do anything wrong. Evie would never cross a line and date someone she worked with. Evie would never find herself framed for a crime she didn't commit.

Rory blinked back the tears burning her eyes. She'd thought she'd left it all behind her—the accusations, the whispers, the "thanks but no, thanks" responses to every job she applied for.

But it was her family's reaction that hurt the worst. Not that they didn't believe she was innocent. But she couldn't shake the feeling they thought she'd somehow brought this on herself. By being too naive, too trusting, too *something*.

"Regardless of what Earl does or doesn't know… I think it would be best if I'm the one who deals with collecting the deposits from now on."

"Evie…" Rory gaped at her cousin, as stunned now as she'd been when Pamela Worthington had confronted her with the "proof" that Rory had been behind the rash of thefts.

"It's not that I don't trust you. You know that."

"Do I?" She couldn't help asking.

Evie lifted her gaze and straightened her shoulders. "You should. But these couples are spending a great deal of money, and it's their trust we can't afford to lose. Besides, collecting deposits falls more into my job description."

That's not the point! The words were on the tip of her tongue, but Evie had already turned back to her computer screen. *I didn't do anything wrong. I didn't deserve to be*

*fired, to be blacklisted from every design firm in South-
ern California!*

But deserved or not, those things had still happened.
Yes, she'd been glad to come to Clearville to help her aunt
Evelyn, but the truth was, she'd slunk out of LA with her
tail between her legs. And now the fallout had followed
her, and Rory felt she had no choice but to duck and run
once more.

She was halfway to the door when Evie asked, "Why
were you looking for Earl, anyway?"

"I'd asked him to fix up the gazebo last week."

"The gazebo?"

For a split second, Evie's gaze lost focus, a sadness
shadowing her expression, and Rory couldn't help wondering if her cousin was thinking about her own plans
for her wedding and the ceremony that was to have taken
place there years ago. And how, back then, it had been
her relationship—and not the gazebo—that had ended up
in shambles.

"It was looking a little worn around the edges, and with
Ryder and Lindsay's wedding coming up…" She shook
her head. "Anyway, it turns out it's in worse shape than I
first thought."

Rory didn't know if Evie picked up on the sympathy in
her voice, but if she did, her cousin knew all too well how
to make people stop feeling sorry for her. "If the gazebo
is in bad shape, that makes it a liability. A—"

"A lawsuit waiting to happen," Rory filled in, recalling
Jamison's words earlier.

Her throbbing ankle echoed its agreement. Not only did
they have to protect their guests, they also had to protect
themselves. If Aunt Evelyn were still in charge, she would
feel the same way Evie did. The two strong businesswomen
didn't have any trouble following their heads. And maybe

they had it right. After all, where had following her heart gotten Rory except into a boatload of trouble?

"Lindsay and Ryder's wedding can still take place as planned," Evie said pragmatically. "They can always use the rose garden."

The garden was lovely. A place where numerous weddings had taken place. But it wasn't the gazebo. It wasn't where Lindsay and Ryder wanted to say their vows. It wasn't where Rory dreamed of having her own ceremony.

Rory wasn't giving up. Not on her dreams of the future and not on the wedding Lindsay and Ryder wanted. "There's still time."

Evie raised a disbelieving eyebrow. "Less than two weeks."

"Like I said," Rory responded with a confidence she didn't entirely feel, "plenty of time."

Her cousin shook her head. "I know you want to believe everything ends in happily-ever-after, but you need to be practical about this. Talk to Ryder and Lindsay about moving the ceremony now. Don't put it off with the hope that a bunch of talking rodents are magically going to fix the place."

Rory offered a quick curtsy. "As you command, my evil queen."

Her cousin rolled her eyes and turned her attention back to her spreadsheet. Evie might not believe in fairy tales, but Rory still did. She wasn't about to lose faith in giving Ryder and Lindsay the wedding of their dreams.

"Ready, Robbie?" Ryder Kincaid called out to his son. "Okay, go long!"

Cocking back the golden arm that had carried him all the way from small-town Clearville to a college football scholarship, Ryder threw a perfect spiral to his son. The ball arced through the late-afternoon summer sky, hitting the boy right in the hands...and then bounding off to land in the sand a few feet away.

Smiling sheepishly behind too-long bangs and pair of wire-rimmed glasses, Robbie scrambled after the pigskin. "Almost had it!"

"So close, bud!" Ryder called back, his smile as wide as if his son had caught the winning touchdown in the Super Bowl. "Kid's smart as a whip. Can't catch to save his life."

Jamison couldn't help thinking the boy's skills would have benefited from playing catch with his dad from the time that he was Hannah's age, instead of just over the past few months. "Maybe if he—"

"Maybe what?" Ryder asked as Robbie chucked the ball back in an end-over-end toss.

"Maybe Robbie takes after Lindsay."

"You got that right." Ryder's grin was just as big as he thought of his fiancée, and Jamison knew he'd made the right decision in not speaking his mind.

Ryder was crazy about Lindsay. That much Jamison could see, but he couldn't understand it.

In the months after he and Monica separated, she'd done everything she could to keep Jamison from seeing Hannah. Canceling visits, conveniently forgetting when he was scheduled to come by the house, insisting Hannah was sick, asleep or any other excuse she could come up with to keep him from seeing his daughter.

He hadn't wanted to fight with Monica. After his parents' endless battles, he'd learned to bury all emotion, knowing even as a kid that anything he said or did would only throw fuel on an already out-of-control fire. He'd retreated into himself, playing the childish game of closing his eyes in the hope no one could see him.

He'd never intended to fall back into that same pattern

with Monica. He'd done his best to ignore her constant complaining, her out-of-control shopping sprees, the way she'd started spending more time out with friends than at home with Hannah. He'd buried himself in his work, not wanting to admit his own marriage was headed down the same rocky path as his parents'. By the time he'd finally opened his eyes, his daughter had grown from a toddler to a little girl he hardly recognized.

He glanced over to where Hannah was playing off away from Robbie and his cousins, building a Leaning Tower of Pisa sandcastle on her own. Was that missing time the reason why he struggled so much to connect with her now? Or was it something more, something lacking in him, that all his relationships seemed destined to fail?

All Jamison knew for sure was that he'd never forgive Monica for keeping Hannah from him for all those months. And if he'd been Ryder, and Lindsay had kept Robbie away from him for years... There was no way.

"I'm sorry we haven't had more time to hang out since you've been here," Ryder said as his older nephew took over and the three boys started a game that looked far more like dodgeball than football. "But we'll have time with Cowboy Days coming up."

Jamison had seen the signs advertising the event during his trips into town. Normally attending a benefit rodeo—any kind of rodeo—would be last on his to-do list. Here in Clearville, it was evidently a can't-miss event, but his response was noncommittal. "We'll see," he told Ryder. "Hannah isn't comfortable in big crowds. And I know you're trying to get as much as you can done before the wedding and honeymoon."

"Yeah, I can't believe the wedding's coming up so soon. But when Rory told us about a cancellation, we couldn't pass up the chance to have the wedding at Hillcrest House even if it did mean putting a rush on things."

"It did happen fast, didn't it?" Jamison couldn't help murmuring. And why was he somehow not surprised Rory had a hand in the abbreviated engagement?

"Depends on how you count. As far as Lindsay, Robbie and I are concerned, we've already waited almost ten years to be a family."

Jamison's gaze cut to Ryder as his friend spoke those words, but no buried anger, no lasting bitterness over the past lingered in his expression. Nothing but excitement and anticipation for the future.

"We're lucky Rory was willing to work with us, and she's done an amazing job with the wedding preparations."

"What's her story, anyway?"

Ryder's eyebrows shot upward. "Seriously? You're interested in Rory McClaren?"

"I didn't say I was interested. I'm...curious. Hannah thinks she's some kind of fairy-tale princess and fairy godmother all rolled into one, and I want to know more about her."

"Well, from what Lindsay says, the woman can perform miracles when it comes to weddings." Ryder shot him a sidelong glance. "It's a pretty sure bet Rory's got plans for her own dream wedding someday."

Jamison felt his face heat. He needed to put on some more damn sunscreen. "Not interested," he repeated, "just curious."

And maybe if he kept telling himself that, he'd start to believe it.

You were thinking of kissing me.

Thinking about it? Jamison still didn't know how he'd escaped her house without pulling her into his arms and tasting those lips that had tempted him from the start.

"Right… About Rory. Her family's owned Hillcrest for years. Her aunt's been running it the past three decades or so, but she recently brought Rory and her cousin Evie in to help out with the wedding destination packages they're promoting. From what I've heard, Rory had been living in LA. She worked for some hotshot interior design firm— the kind that decorates houses for Hollywood stars and stages million-dollar mansions for putting them up to sell."

Jamison could picture Rory in the role—dream weddings, dream houses, all part of her belief in happily-ever-after. "Sounds like a job she'd be good at."

"Yeah, well…"

"What?" Jamison asked when his friend's voice trailed off.

Ryder shook his head. "Small-town gossip about the reason why Rory was let go from the job. Like you said, not a whole lot else to do around here."

"Hey, Uncle Ryder, catch!" One of the boys tossed the ball back, an end-over-end lame duck Ryder still managed to deflect up into the air at the last minute and catch one-handed—much to his nephew's delight.

Ryder grinned as he spun the ball between his hands, cocked back his arm and returned the ball in a perfect spiral.

"Show-off," Jamison muttered under his breath, more annoyed by his burning curiosity about the gossip about Rory than he was by his friend reliving his golden years.

It was hard to imagine any scandal connected to Rory McClaren. She had such a sweetness, such an air of innocence surrounding her. But he'd seen a hint of the shadows hiding behind her wide blue eyes.

If his marriage to Monica had taught him anything, it was that everyone had secrets. Had he paid more attention in the final months of his marriage, maybe he would have seen what was coming. Maybe he could have stopped her, and if he had—

Jamison looked over at his daughter, carefully crafting her sandcastle, the expression on her sweet face so serious, even as the boys yelled and laughed and raced around her.

Maybe if he had, Hannah's mother would still be alive.

"What can I say?" Ryder raised a shoulder in a negligent shrug. "Some of us have still got it. Hey, man, you okay?"

Jamison pulled in a deep breath. He couldn't close his eyes and pretend everything was going to be okay. If Rory was going to be in his—in *Hannah's* life—even for a short time, then he needed to learn everything he could about her. For his daughter's sake.

"You were telling me about Rory and her life in LA."

"Oh, yeah. Look, I'm sure it was nothing, but the story goes that she got involved with the boss's son and it didn't end well." Ryder shook his head. "As someone who once worked for his in-laws, I can sympathize. I guess things got pretty ugly at the end, with lots of accusations being thrown around about Rory stealing some stuff...not that I believe it for a second."

The whole thing sounded rather petty and ridiculous. What had Rory done—refused to return the gifts her ex had given her? Kept some of the things he'd left at her place? Ryder was right. The rumors were likely nothing more than a bad breakup blown out of proportion thanks to the Clearville grapevine.

"Has Rory talked to you about the gazebo?"

"She said it's in bad shape and even asked if she could hire me to do the work, but with trying to get our scheduled jobs finished—" Ryder shook his head "—I don't see how I can squeeze another project in. Lindsay's disappointed, but she understands. Plus, Rory's done such a fabulous job on short notice that she doesn't want to make her feel bad."

The image of blue eyes flashing wide with hurt and dis-appointment jabbed at Jamison's conscience. *He* had made Rory feel bad, snapping at her the way he had when she'd been nothing short of amazing with Hannah.

And before Jamison realized what he was saying, he told his friend, "I could do it."

"Do what?"

"Fix up the gazebo."

"Seriously? You haven't done any remodeling work in years. I bet a judge's gavel is the closest thing to a hammer you've been around since we were in college."

Although it was quite possibly the worst idea he'd ever had, Jamison insisted. "It'll all come back to me the min-ute I put on a tool belt."

The two of them had met while working construction part-time. Despite the differences in their backgrounds and the fact that Jamison was a few years older than Ryder, they had struck up an instant friendship.

And it was that friendship that had him saying, "Con-sider the gazebo your wedding present."

That was the reason he'd made the offer. It had to be. No way should he be doing this as a way for Rory to see him as some kind of hero when nothing could be further from the truth. He was simply helping out a friend.

Nothing more.

Right. Helping out Ryder by fixing up Rory's favorite place in the whole, whole world.

A wide grin split his friend's face. "Hot da—dog!" he exclaimed with a glance at the kids. "You have made my day. No, my wedding! Lindsay is going to be thrilled, and this is much better than some high-tech coffee maker or-dered off the bridal registry!"

His face heated at how closely his friend had him pegged. A perfectly wrapped present had been delivered to the hotel the other day, compliments of his assistant's efficiency. He had no idea what the box contained or even what the card said. "I would never buy something so lame."

"Are you sure about this, though? Isn't the point of this vacation for you to spend time with Hannah?"

Jamison rubbed at the back of his neck. "I'm going a little stir-crazy here, Ry. I'm used to nonstop meetings and calls and conferences. This is all getting to me."

Restlessness and frustration stacked one on top of the other inside him, like the brightly colored blocks Hannah used to play with. Higher and higher until a crash was inevitable. He had too much time on his hands. Too much time to worry about Hannah. Too much time to—

You were thinking of kissing me.

"Right…" his friend drawled. "I can see how tough this is, you know, when life is literally a walk on the beach. Tell the truth—you've been dying to check your phone the whole time we've been out here."

"There's no reception," Jamison grumbled as Ryder laughed. "Doesn't it drive you crazy? This small-town living?"

"This small-town living has given me the chance to know my son."

"You could have done that in San Francisco," he argued even as Ryder pinned him with another knowing look.

"I'm not that far removed from the corporate world, Jamie," he said, breaking out the childhood nickname only Jamison's father still used and only to remind him of who he used to be. "You can't tell me you'd be doing this in San Francisco." His friend tipped his head toward the kids running along the windblown beach.

"I have a job," Jamison argued. "A career—"

A child. One he'd already let down so many times in her short life.

With his gaze locked on Hannah and her precarious sandcastle, Jamison admitted, "I don't know if I can do this, Ry."

His friend was silent for a moment before he advised, "Do your best, Jamison. That's all any of us can do as parents."

Jamison nodded as his friend clapped him on the shoulder before jogging over to join the boys in their game. *Do your best...* Good advice, but other than in his professional life, doing his best had never been enough. Not for his mother, who tried to fill the emptiness in their lives with one failed marriage after another. Not for Monica, who'd taken to wild spending sprees and late-night partying with friends during the final months of *their* failed marriage. And not for Hannah, who would grow up without a mother thanks to the choices he had made.

You're her father. Rory's gentle yet insistent voice seemed to echo in the ocean breeze at his back, a warm, buffeting push in his daughter's direction. *She's still a little girl who wants to run and laugh and play again...*

"Hey, Hannah Banana," he said as she upended another bucket of wet dark sand to start another tower of her leaning castle. "Can I give you a hand?"

She squinted up at him in the sunshine, her sweet face adorably wrinkled, and Jamison stepped to the side so his shadow blocked the glare. "I dunno. Do you know how to play?"

His own father had taught him how to fix, repair, build any number of projects. How to start with the best materials and use the right tool to guarantee what he crafted was solid, sturdy, dependable. Built to last...

But when it came to forming lasting relationships—with his father, his mother, Monica...Hannah—Jamison felt as though every foundation rested on shifting, unstable sand, always ready to give way at any moment.

I have faith in you.

Rory's words rang in his ears. He didn't have that kind of faith in himself. But maybe he didn't need to. Maybe for now, for as long as he was in Clearville, Rory's faith in him would be enough…

Sinking down onto his knees in the cold, damp sand by his daughter's side, he brushed some dried grains from her pink cheek. "I was thinking maybe you could teach me."

Chapter Seven

"As you can see, the rose garden is a beautiful spot for a wedding. In fact, we have a ceremony scheduled here in a few days." Rory forced a smile as she turned her gaze to the young couple who'd come to tour Hillcrest.

The rose garden was beautiful, and if they had to move Lindsay and Ryder's wedding to this location, the ceremony would still be as touching and emotional as it would be taking place in the gazebo. But it wouldn't be the wedding Lindsay and Ryder had imagined, and that was the problem. Rory wanted to give every couple the wedding of their dreams, not some kind of runner-up.

The couple exchanged a glance. "On the website, we saw pictures of a gazebo. It looked like the perfect backdrop. We'd love to see it in person."

Her heart sinking, Rory admitted, "I'm sorry. The gazebo isn't available at the moment. We have some renovations in the works. I'm sure it won't be long before the work is completed, and there's still plenty of time before the two of you plan to get married. For now, why don't we take a look inside at the ballroom?"

Twenty minutes later, the young couple left...without signing a contract. It was a big decision, and Hillcrest House wasn't the only option for couples looking to get married, but Rory couldn't help feeling like she'd failed. Again.

She'd hated having to call Ryder to tell him about the sorry shape the gazebo was in, but in the back of her mind, she'd hoped he might have a crew she could hire. Evie would blow a gasket if she learned Rory had tried to solicit a Hillcrest groom to do manual labor at the hotel, but construction work *was* Ryder's job. But he was also in high demand, booked solid and rushing to get several jobs completed before he left on his honeymoon.

He had told her he would see what he could do, but Rory hadn't heard back, and her other efforts to find someone on such short notice had turned up empty. She didn't want to admit defeat, but maybe Evie was right. Maybe she needed to be practical—and not just about the gazebo.

She hadn't seen Jamison and Hannah in the past two days, and she hated how much she missed them. More than once, she'd done a double take when she spotted a dark-haired man out of the corner of her eye or stopped midsentence at the sound of a child's voice only to be disappointed that it wasn't the man or the child she was instinctively looking for.

She was getting too close, too fast. She'd made the same mistake with Peter, certain she could overcome the obstacles between them and trying to make molehills out of mountains. She'd fallen hard—and landed even harder. If she wasn't careful, when Jamison and Hannah returned home after the wedding, she'd be left behind nursing something far more painful than a bruised ankle.

If only Evie's "be practical" advice didn't feel so much like quitting without trying her best. How could she give up on having the gazebo ready for Ryder and Lindsay's wedding before she'd exhausted every possibility of getting it fixed?

And how was saving herself from heartache later more practical if it meant being miserable now?

Rory was still waging that internal battle as she headed for Evie's office, tucked back behind the registration desk. A group of hotel employees had gathered over to the side near an empty luggage rack, and Rory recognized the tall redhead in the middle.

Trisha Katzman had worked at the hotel for years. The thirtysomething woman had made it clear she, and not Rory, should have been the one to take on the expanded wedding coordinator role. Rory had done her best to smooth things over, to reassure Trisha she wasn't taking over her job and the increase in weddings would create more than enough work—and reward for a job well done—for everyone.

Her efforts had met with little success. The redhead was coldly polite face-to-face, but Rory could feel the daggers the other woman shot her way the second her back was turned.

And something had changed lately. The subtle disgruntled looks were no longer so subtle, and Trisha's smug expression reminded Rory of her last miserable months in LA.

The other women in Trisha's clique returned Rory's greeting before picking up their conversation. "I still can't believe that store's computer got hacked and some loser stole my credit card number," one of them was complaining as she walked by.

The other two made sympathetic sounds, but Trisha pointedly looked over her shoulder, tracking Rory's movements as she said, "Hard to know who to trust these days, isn't it?"

Rory froze.

She knew.

The patterned carpet shifted beneath her feet as her stomach listed and sank. Rory didn't know how the other woman had found out about what happened in LA, but she had no doubt Trisha was responsible for the rumors swirling around the hotel.

Once Rory would have walked over and confronted the group. She'd learned back in junior high that showing fear in front of a group of mean girls was the worst thing she could do. But after everything that happened in LA, when nothing she said made any difference and keeping silent had ended up her only defense, the words stuck in her throat.

Ducking her head, Rory headed away from the group and down the narrow hallway to Evie's office. Her cousin glanced up at her quick knock. "Oh, good. I was about to come looking for you—what's wrong?"

"It's—nothing." Rory didn't need to see the "I told you so" look in her cousin's eyes. She'd been fooling herself thinking she could have a fresh start in a place she'd always loved.

Evie's gaze narrowed, but she didn't press. "Good, because right now we have enough trouble. Mrs. Broderick called. She swears she and her daughter requested veal *piccata* and not chicken as part of the reception menu."

"They went back and forth before deciding on chicken." Rory specifically remembered. The conversation had gone on so long, by the time the two women made up their minds, she thought she might scream if she heard the words *veal*, *chicken* or *piccata* ever again.

Evie lifted an eyebrow. "That's not what she says."

"I'll talk to the chef. Hopefully it won't be too late to cancel the order."

"And if it is? They signed the contract, which states chicken," her cousin pointed out. "If you talk to them…"

"What difference would that make?" If Mrs. Broderick didn't believe what was in front of her in black and white, what was the likelihood the woman would believe anything Rory had to say?

"Then I'll talk to them," Evie decided.

"No, Evie, this is my job. I'll handle it."

Rory held her breath, waiting for her cousin to take yet another responsibility away from her because she couldn't be trusted—

Finally, her cousin gave a short nod. "All right."

Half an hour later, after dealing with their disgruntled chef and butcher, Rory stepped outside. She inhaled a deep breath, taking in the scents of forest pine and salty ocean and hoping the combination would clear her head.

She had a dozen phone calls and emails to return on everything from placing orders with the florist to confirming the chairs and bunting with the rental company to sending a new song list to the band for a wedding. But nothing needed to be done right that second. And with Trisha and her clique still inside the lobby, Rory wanted a few minutes to herself.

But as she followed the meandering walkways leading from the hotel, she didn't take the curve that would lead toward her cottage. Instead, she found herself walking down the tree-lined path toward the gazebo.

Her steps slowed on the flagstone steps, not wanting to

see the caution tape she'd asked one of the groundskeepers to put up, cordoning off the damaged and dangerous steps.

It was a simple wooden structure. Her hopes and dreams for a future and a family with a man she loved were not tied into its decorative pillars or carved eaves. Even if it might feel that way...

"Miss Rory!"

Her mood lifted, concerns about Trisha and the gazebo melting away when she saw Hannah tugging on Jamison's hand as the father-daughter duo headed her way. Maybe she should have been worried how happy the simple sight of them made her, but Rory had never been one to question a good thing. She'd always been more inclined to embrace it—easy enough to do when Hannah broke free the last few steps and threw her arms around her legs.

Bending down to return her hug, Rory breathed in the scent of little girl, baby shampoo and sunshine. Words spilled out of Hannah as she filled Rory in on the past two days—time spent going into town, including an all-important trip to the café for a cookie, and a day at the beach.

"Me and Daddy builded a sandcastle this big!" Hannah threw her arms out wide, and Rory met Jamison's gaze for the first time.

"You did?"

"We *built* a sandcastle," he automatically corrected.

"Daddy," Hannah sighed, "I just tol' her that. And it was this big!"

"Well, I am very proud of you," Rory said, her words not for Hannah alone, something Jamison picked up on based by the eye roll he gave her.

She had a hard time imagining Jamison on the beach, let alone playing with his daughter in the sand. And yet she could see a hint of sun in his cheeks and on the forearms left bare by the shirtsleeves he'd pushed up to his elbows. She wouldn't go so far as to say he looked relaxed—his silver eyes were too intense, too watchful to fit that description—but he did seem more at ease than when he'd arrived at the hotel.

He was even dressed more casually in a faded gray Henley and jeans. The comfortable clothes molded to his broad shoulders and muscular legs and had Rory wishing he would sweep her up into his arms again…and not because she'd injured her ankle.

As if reading her mind, he asked, "How's the ankle?"

Rory lifted her leg. "Almost as good as new. The scratches are healing and the bruises are already starting to fade…" It hadn't been her intention to draw Jamison's gaze to her legs or the strappy white sandals she was wearing despite the still-tender ankle, but she couldn't argue the results or the masculine appreciation in his expression.

"Toilet paper must have done the trick."

The wry humor in his voice did as much to set the butterflies in her stomach fluttering as the heat in his gaze. "I couldn't agree more."

"I'm glad you're all better, Miss Rory, 'cause me and Daddy have a surprise!"

"Hannah, you're not supposed to tell her. That's what makes it a surprise."

Her big brown eyes wide with innocence, Hannah protested, "But I didn't tell her, Daddy! I didn't tell her about fixing—oops!" The little girl clapped her dimpled hands over her mouth to keep the words from spilling out.

Rory laughed. "Okay, well, someone needs to tell me! What are the two of you up to?"

With a nod at his daughter, Jamison said, "Go ahead."

Throwing her hands out wide, she exclaimed, "Daddy's gonna fix the playhouse!"

Rory looked from the exuberance written across Hannah's face to her father's much harder to read expression. "Fix... You mean the gazebo?" she asked, her voice filled with disbelief. And then even more disbelief as she asked, "You?"

But if she'd offended Jamison, he didn't let it show as he stepped closer and bent his head toward hers. "What's the matter? You don't think I'm up for the job?"

A day or two ago, she might have said no, but in the T-shirt and jeans, he looked the part of a calendar-worthy handyman. This ruggedly physical side of him was something Rory would never have imagined. So different from the cool, composed lawyer. Add a tool belt and a hammer swung over one broad shoulder and—

She had to stop herself right there. No need for a hammer when her heart was doing all the pounding.

"I'm sure you're—" Rory snapped her mouth shut, his turn of phrase getting stuck in her throat. Feeling a rush of heat rise in her cheeks, she finished, "Perfectly capable."

Desperate to ignore the glint in his eyes that said he knew what she was thinking even if it wasn't what she was saying, she said, "But I don't understand—"

"I was talking with Ryder, and I offered to fix the gazebo. You know, for their wedding."

"Oh, Jamison..."

As if hearing the wobble of tears in her voice, he quickly went on. "Ryder's going to provide any of the materials or tools I need so long as I swear not to cut my fool hand, foot or head off."

Rory laughed in return even if she was still blinking back tears. "You're not, um, likely to actually do any of those things, are you?"

"It hasn't been that long since I had my hands on a power tool."

There was nothing overtly sexual about that statement,

but Rory had to pull her gaze away from the muscular arms and chest his T-shirt put on display. Definitely some powerful tools there, but it was his offer—his thoughtfulness—that had her throwing her arms around his neck.

"I can't believe you'd do this. It is so sweet of you."

He started, caught off guard by her impetuous hug before wrapping his arms around her waist. "It's hard, sweaty, manly work. Nothing sweet about it."

"You're helping give your friends the wedding of their dreams."

"Don't you dare call me Ryder's fairy godfather. I'd never live it down." His wry smile faded as he pulled back far enough to meet her gaze. "Besides, I'm not just doing this for him."

"No?"

Rory counted out the time it took for him to respond by the rapid beating of her heart. "No." He frowned as if annoyed by his own admission. "I'm doing this for you."

She sucked in a quick breath. "For me?"

"You know," he clarified, "for all the help you've given me with Hannah."

"Oh. You don't owe me for that, Jamison." She took a step back, brushing at the material of her full skirt where it clung to his denim-covered thigh. She could have used the reminder that he was a guest—a member of the wedding party—before she'd thrown herself into his arms.

She turned her focus to Hannah, who'd wandered a few feet down the path toward the rose garden. "I've enjoyed spending time with her, and since she's one of my flower girls, it's part of the job."

"Is it?" he challenged. "Because if that's the truth, then maybe I'm the one imagining things."

"Imagining things..."

His hand closed around her wrist, trapping her palm

against the muscular strength of his thigh. "Yeah, like that you're thinking of kissing me right now."

Her breath caught in her throat, and her fingers instinctively flexed, her nails digging into warm denim. Jamison's eyes darkened from silver to steel and suddenly she was imagining so much more than kissing—

"But we still can't," she echoed his words from the other day.

Can't, not *didn't want to*, because, oh, how she wanted to.

Without taking his eye off her, Jamison called out to his daughter. "Hey, Hannah, how'd you like to play a game of hide-and-seek? Close your eyes and count to one hundred."

"One hundred?" she asked as Hannah's singsong voice filled the air.

"She only knows up to twenty."

Turning her wrist until her hand clasped his, Rory tugged Jamison toward the closest tree. "Then we better make this fast."

She was already breathless with anticipation by the time they circled around the large pine, and he hadn't even touched her. By the time he pulled her into his arms, Rory thought her heart might explode. Yet despite her instructions to hurry, Jamison didn't kiss like a man in a rush.

He kissed like a man who'd traveled far and had finally, at long last, come home. Like a man who'd thought of nothing else, who had dreamed only of this moment. He caught her bottom lip, tugging in a gentle tease, before delving farther. His tongue swept inside, and her senses reeled, spinning off into a world she'd never known existed.

A world of pleasure. A world of sensation. So bright and startling all else seemed dull and gray.

And Rory had to have more.

Digging her hands into his dark hair, she pulled him closer. Arousal poured through her veins, centering low in her belly and striking sparks wherever their bodies touched. But the contact, her mouth eagerly seeking his, her breasts straining against his chest, wasn't enough. She had to have more and almost cried out in protest when Jamison broke the kiss.

"Rory," he ground out, words barely registering beyond the pulse pounding in her ears, "we better stop…"

Though the haze of desire, Rory heard Hannah's voice. On a breathless whisper, she said, "We still have ten seconds left."

"Nine," Jamison corrected, his breath warm against her skin as he trailed kisses down the length of her throat.

Her head fell back in pure pleasure. She thought she just might melt into the rough bark of the tree at her back, but Jamison pulled her tight and she melted into him instead. "Nine?" she asked weakly.

"Hannah always skips fifteen."

Sure enough, the little girl missed the number, and Rory started her own countdown. "Four, three…"

Recognizing the challenge, Jamison covered her mouth with his in the hottest, fastest kiss of Rory's life. One that left her gasping for air even as Hannah yelled out, "Twenty!" and started to search for them.

Ready or not.

Rory stepped back and sucked in a single lungful of air that wasn't superheated by the attraction burning between them before Hannah rushed around the tree and stopped short at the sight of them.

"Daddy, you're s'posed to hide." Shaking her head in disappointment, she said, "You and Miss Rory aren't very good at this game."

Jamison met Rory's gaze, and beneath the shared amusement was enough heat to set another round of fireworks shooting off in her stomach. Rory didn't want to argue with a four-year-old, but this game was one Jamison was very good at.

As it turned out, Jamison was quite as bad at hide-and-seek as his daughter feared. That wasn't as much of a surprise as the enjoyment he found in the game. Of course, part of that was the grown-up version he and Rory were playing—stealing kisses while Hannah's eyes were closed, finding a hiding spot of their own before tracking the little girl down in the rose garden.

But they'd both been careful to keep those stolen moments lighter, more playful. Not that the spark had dimmed. If anything, it built with every touch, every glance.

A controlled burn instead of an out-and-out wildfire like their first kiss.

"You know, I was so excited earlier—" Catching sight of his raised eyebrows, Rory rolled her eyes, but not before her cheeks turned a flattering shade of pink. "About the *gazebo*," she stressed, "that I didn't ask what you plan to do about Hannah while you're working."

Hannah had skipped ahead on the flagstone path only to get distracted by a colorful butterfly flitting by. The joy and awe on her sweet face brought a lump of emotion to the back of his throat. He'd seen his daughter break free and spread her wings over the past few days, and he was terrified of doing anything that would send her back into the cocoon of sadness and loss.

"I talked to Ryder about hiring a teenage girl they've used before."

Seeming to remember how reluctant his daughter sometimes was to leave his side, Rory asked, "Do you think Hannah will be okay with someone new watching her?"

"I hope so. If not—" Then he might soon have bigger problems than finding time to fix the gazebo.

"Does she have a babysitter back home she's comfortable with?"

"I haven't used any sitters back home…not since before the accident. Hannah's been staying with her grandparents. With everything that was going on, it seemed better that way."

"She's here with you now. That's what matters."

"Yeah." He sighed. "She's with me for now."

"For now," Rory echoed, "but not for long? Is that what you're saying? What happens when you go back to San Francisco, Jamison?"

Even though she'd asked the question, the disappointment in her expression said she knew the answer as well as he did. "Monica's parents want Hannah to live with them."

And they didn't even know about the promotion, one that would mean long days and even longer nights. Times when he would be leaving for work while Hannah was still asleep in the morning and wouldn't be home until after she was in bed in the evening.

"Hannah's grandmother is a retired nurse. She can be with her all day, every day. And Hannah loves her grandparents. After Monica and I separated, Hannah spent as much time with them as she did with Monica. And far more time than she spent with me."

Something Louisa was quick to point out. He carried around plenty of guilt on his own and didn't need his in-laws piling on, but Louisa knew what button to push—reminding him what a detached and absent father he'd been even before he and Monica separated. And now that Hannah needed him to be both mother and father…

"I'm sure they do love her, but Jamison, you're her father and your daughter needs you. I'm not trying to compare what I went through to Hannah losing her mother, but after Chance's accident, I needed my parents, too. As an adult, I get it. They could only handle so much, and almost all of their time and energy was focused on Chance getting better. But for me, as a kid, I felt like they were as lost to me as Chance was in that coma."

Even after so many years, Jamison picked up on the tremor in Rory's voice, the whisper of a little girl who'd gone unnoticed, unheard. He hated thinking of her feeling that way. Hated thinking of *Hannah* feeling that way.

"Rory—" He swallowed against a lump in his throat. "I—I just want what's best for her."

"I know. I see that, Jamison. I do." The certainty in her gaze turned sorrowful as she added, "What I don't understand is why you don't think that would be you."

Rory knew she shouldn't have been surprised when Jamison didn't answer her question. Just because he'd kissed her senseless didn't mean he was going to spill his guts. And just because she'd poured out the old ache in her heart when she spoke of the horrible days following Chance's accident didn't mean Jamison would pour out his.

Instead, his expression closed off, reminding her of the man she'd first met and not of the man she'd just kissed. Avoiding the emotional discussion, he'd gotten down to the business of inspecting the gazebo. Or at least trying to with Hannah hanging by his side, wanting to "help."

"Got it, Hannah?" he asked, as he ran a measuring tape along the length of the gazebo railing. "Are you holding on tight?"

"Got it, Daddy!" Stretched up on her tippy toes, Hannah held on to one end of the tape.

Jamison jotted down some figures in the small notebook he'd pulled from his pocket. "Okay, kiddo. You can let it go."

Hannah released the small tab and the yellow metal tape zipped back into the casing, bringing a giggle from the little girl and drawing a smile from Jamison, but the shadows lingering in his expression made Rory's heart hurt.

Did he think Hannah would break if he were to unbend enough to hug her—or was he afraid that he would? His love for the little girl was obvious, but so was the fear.

He needed more time. Time with Hannah, not time spent fixing the gazebo. As touched as she was by his offer to help his friend, to help *her*, his daughter needed him far more than Ryder and Lindsay needed the perfect setting for their wedding.

Swallowing against the lump of disappointment in her throat, she opened her mouth, but Hannah beat her to the punch.

"Did ya see, Miss Rory?" The little girl bounced on her toes. "I'm being a big helper!"

Rory met Hannah's wide smile with one of her own as the perfect solution bloomed. "I did see, Hannah. You are such a good helper, and I just had the best idea ever!"

Chapter Eight

Maybe it was something in the water.

Something that made him say yes to harebrained schemes and even come up with a few of his own. Bad enough he'd offered to fix up the gazebo, but what the hell was he thinking yesterday when he agreed to let Rory and Hannah help?

I just had the best idea ever!

Rory's eyes had glimmered with such hope that Jamison had found himself holding his breath in a combination of dread and anticipation. Even before she started talking, he'd had a feeling that whatever the crazy idea swirling in her pretty little head was, he was going to hate it. And an even worse feeling that whatever it was, he was going to be fool enough to agree to it. Just to keep that light in her eyes and the smile on her face...

Jamison fought back a groan as he and Hannah made their way down the flagstone path. He adjusted the tool belt at his waist even as he gave serious thought to smacking himself upside the head with a hammer. How was he supposed to work and keep an eye on his daughter...when he couldn't keep his eyes off Rory?

He'd reached for his phone a dozen times already, prepared to call Rory and then Ryder and tell them both the whole thing was off. He could tell his friend the work was too much and the ceremony could take place in the rose garden with Lindsay and the guests none the wiser.

There was only one problem.

"I'm going to be a big help, right, Daddy?"

Even if Ryder was smart enough to keep his mouth shut with the woman in his life, Jamison had already blown it by telling the pint-size girl in his.

Excitement radiated from her tiny body as she bounced by his side, jumping from one flagstone to the next, one hand holding the oversize yellow hard hat on her head.

"I get to help Miss Rory fix the playhouse."

"It's a gazebo," he corrected. "And I'll be the one fixing it," he added before realizing he sounded like a total jerk.

In the months since Monica's death, Jamison couldn't think of a single suggestion he'd come up with that Hannah hadn't met with *I don't want to.* Even her favorite activities back home—going to the park or the zoo—had all been shot down.

But not this chance to work on the gazebo.

Did it matter that Rory was the bigger draw when it came to Hannah wanting to lend a hand? Wasn't his daughter's happiness, no matter the reason, most important?

And what happens when you go back home? When there is no Rory around to add a hint of sweetness to everything she touches and to make more than smiley-face oatmeal happy?

Construction wasn't easy work, and Jamison had had

his share of injuries—the worst of them a pair of broken ribs and a punctured lung thanks to a fall through some rotten floorboards. But the sharp pain and struggle to breathe were nothing compared to what he felt when he thought of trying to care for Hannah on his own.

"But we get to help, right, Daddy?"

"Sure thing, Hannah Banana. I need all the help I can get," he sighed, wishing the words weren't so blatantly true.

And that was why he found himself trailing after his daughter as she raced ahead toward the gazebo.

"Hi, Miss Rory!" Hannah cried out as she rounded the curve in the path.

Jamison should have been prepared, thanks to his daughter's early-warning signal, yet somehow he was still caught off guard. Because standing in front of the gazebo, gazing up at the aging structure as if the rotting wood and cracked paint had already been stripped away and restored to its once-gleaming glory, Rory turned to greet them with a brilliant smile.

"Look, Miss Rory! We both have hard hats!" Hannah clamped both hands on top of hers as if expecting her sheer excitement to blow the thing right off her head at any second.

And Jamison couldn't help feeling like he should hold on to his own, considering how the sight of Rory in a pair of faded skintight jeans and a pink—hot-pink—hard hat was threatening to blow his mind.

"I see!" And then meeting his gaze over his daughter's hard hat, Rory shot him a wink. "Safety first, right, Jamison? After all, it has been a while…"

She had no idea. If she had, she would have brought a fire extinguisher instead. Something in the intensity of his gaze must have given him away because her smile faded.

His heartbeat quickened as the awareness between them grew. Try as he might, he couldn't keep his eyes from drifting down her body.

He'd never seen her dressed so casually—couldn't have imagined her wearing denim, a fitted white T-shirt, that outlined her breasts far too clearly for his comfort, and honest-to-God work boots. And yet there she was, like some kind of construction worker Barbie.

"This is never going to work," he mumbled under his breath.

Despite the rush of color blooming in her cheeks, Rory pretended she hadn't heard him. She waved a hand at a shaded area several yards away from the gazebo where a picnic basket and blanket waited. "Are you ready to get started, Miss Hannah?" At his daughter's nod, she said, "We have a big bucket of screws and nails we need to separate so all the same sizes are in their own little cups. And then we'll use scissors to cut sandpaper to the right size to fit your daddy's super noisy sander.

"When we're done with that, we have paper and pencils and paint so we can draw pictures of the gazebo and practice on them until your daddy is ready for us to help him paint the real thing. And then we can make sandwiches with the stuff I brought in that basket over there, because all that hard, hard work is going to make us all hungry. What do you think?"

Jamison shook his head. He thought she was amazing. All those little projects would keep Hannah engaged and entertained. And he never would have thought of any of them. Somehow, though, instead of his inadequacies as a father casting a dark pall over his mood, gratitude rushed through him.

He caught Rory's hand as she walked by and gazed down at her in that ridiculous hat. Her blue eyes sparkled and her pale pink lips curved in a smile that had him thinking about their kiss...

She might not have been dressed like one, but he couldn't help asking, "Are you sure you aren't some kind of magical fairy-tale princess?"

"Why, Jamison, I didn't think you believed in fairy tales."

"I don't," he insisted. "But I believe in you. You have this way of making things—even the most everyday, average things—special."

And if that wasn't magic, then he didn't know what was.

Despite Jamison's initial concerns over the shape of the gazebo, a more thorough inspection revealed the overall structure—the support beams, most of the main floor and the roof—was sound. The steps, the lattice facade and the railing needed the most work, but he'd assured her the repairs were all doable and could be fixed before the wedding.

With Hannah occupied on the blanket with some of the little games she'd come up with, Rory had worked at Jamison's side, hoping effort made up for what she lacked in experience.

"Admit it...you're impressed." Rory pointed a plastic water bottle Jamison's way as they took a short break.

He gave his typical snort of disbelief as he raised his own bottle. But before he took a long swallow, he murmured, "Only every time we're together."

She took a quick sip of the cool liquid, thinking it might do her more good to dump the whole thing over her head. Her heated thoughts at watching Jamison do something as simple as drink from a bottle didn't bode well for completing the gazebo without her jumping his bones.

I believe in you.

How long had it been since someone had that kind of faith in her? Months? Years?

Evie had always been the practical one, Chance the adventurous one and Rory the dreamer. The girl with her head in the clouds, whose ideas were always too impractical, too over-the-top, too silly to be taken seriously.

But Jamison believed in her.

With Hannah close by, they had no chance to repeat the kiss from the day before. But the little girl's presence wasn't enough to keep Rory's thoughts from straying in that direction or to keep her from imagining Jamison felt the same way.

More than once, their gazes had locked over some small task—their fingers brushing as he handed her the hammer, his chest pressing against her shoulder as he reached around her to help with a particular stubborn nail, his breath against her neck raising gooseflesh on her skin as he offered some words of instruction.

"You told me you're a jill-of-all-trades, but this seems a bit much for a wedding coordinator."

"Well, I wasn't always a wedding coordinator," she told him, only to instantly regret it. She didn't want to talk about LA. Didn't want to think about Pamela or Peter or the thefts she'd been accused of.

"So what did you do before this?" Jamison asked.

"I worked for an interior design firm." She forced a smile. "Way too girlie for you to find interesting."

"Still not sure how carpentry falls under interior designer... And for the record, I happen to find girlie very interesting."

His appreciative glance coaxed a genuine smile out of her, and she sighed. "I started at the bottom with big dreams of working my way up. As low designer on the totem pole, I was stuck with all the jobs no one wanted—

including getting my hands dirty to get a remodel done on time. If that meant ripping out carpet because the subcontractor no-showed or repainting an entire kitchen because the client changed her mind at the last minute and the painter had already walked off the job, then I was their girl."

"So what happened?"

Rory started. "What makes you think something happened?"

Jamison shrugged casually. "You're here, aren't you? Something must have happened."

"I had the chance to work at Hillcrest with my family. This place means so much to me, I wouldn't have missed that for the world." Even if she hadn't been without a job and weeks from running out of rent money for the ridiculously expensive studio she'd called home.

"So...no heartbroken guy left behind?"

"Heartbroken? Definitely not."

"But there *was* a guy."

Rory squeezed the water bottle, the thin plastic crackling in her hands. "His name was Peter, and he's the boss's son. I should have known better than to get involved with someone at work." But some lessons were hard to learn. By no means could she classify her relationship with Jamison as strictly professional.

"Pamela, his mother, had far greater aspirations for him than dating a lowly assistant in her company. I tried not to let it bother me, and Peter assured me his mother would come around. All I had to do was to give her some time."

"But that didn't work?"

"The longer we dated, the more uncomfortable things became at work. I don't think it was coincidence that I was always assigned to the most difficult clients. My friends all thought I should quit, but—I don't know. I guess I was too stubborn and the job wasn't the problem. Quitting wouldn't make my relationship with Pamela any easier. If anything, it would have proved to her that I could be run off."

"And you weren't willing to give up on Peter."

"I thought he was the one. So I put up with so much crap from his mother. She'd turned a job I loved into one I hated. I dreaded waking up in the morning, knowing I'd have to do battle with that dragon, but I did it. I did it for months, because I told myself it was worth it. I was willing to fight for our relationship, but Peter…"

The worst of her ex's betrayal caught in her throat, as did the humiliating circumstances that had led to her leaving LA. She should tell Jamison the entire story, she knew she should, but—

I believe in you.

She didn't want to lose the faith he had in her, not when it meant so much, not when there was a chance he *wouldn't* believe in her once she told him the whole truth.

"Looks like someone's ready for a nap."

Lying back on the picnic blanket, his eyes closed to the bright, cloudless sky overhead, Jamison said, "You have no idea."

Muscles he hadn't used in years groaned in protest at the slightest movement, thanks to the hard work he'd put in over the past three days, but Jamison was determined to have the gazebo ready by Ryder's wedding. If he had to throw in the towel, his friend would never let him hear the end of it.

Rory's low chuckle brushed over his skin on the warm summer breeze. "Like father, like daughter."

He cracked an eye open to see Hannah slumped to one side, half-eaten peanut butter and jelly sandwich in hand.

She looked angelic, peaceful. Pushing up onto his elbows, he said, "It's hard work being a number one helper."

The title was one his daughter wore with pride, overcoming her shyness with strangers to tell anyone who would listen—the big, burly guy at the lumberyard, the skinny teen in the paint department, the gum-popping cashier at the hardware store—that she was the best helper ever.

He'd had his doubts about taking Hannah along on those trips, certain he could get in and out much faster and more efficiently on his own, but Rory had insisted. And since he seemed incapable of saying no to either of them, the two ladies had accompanied him. And yeah, maybe it had taken more time, but it was time spent with Hannah…and with Rory. She'd pushed Hannah around in a basket, managing to turn even the countless trips up and down the aisles in the huge home improvement store while he looked for the right L-bracket into some kind of adventure.

"When will we be ready for the big reveal?"

"I'm sure we'll be done at least an hour before the rehearsal dinner next Friday."

Rory tossed a crumpled napkin at him. "Very funny."

He grinned as the wadded-up ball sailed past without hitting its mark. Despite having to work around Hannah's nap time and Rory's scheduled fittings, tasting and meetings with clients and potential clients, they'd made real progress.

They'd torn out the splintering lattice fasciae and trim, and pried up the rotted steps and any warped boards on the circular platform. He'd cut the replacement boards and had spent the morning sanding them smooth, filling the air with the slight scent of burning wood. A fine layer of sawdust covered just about everything. Including Rory's toned arms, left bare by the pink-and-white-striped tank top she wore.

Suddenly not feeling so tired, he could think of better things to do while Hannah slept than to take a nap of his own...

"So tell me the story," Rory said, catching Jamison off guard.

Talking wasn't where his mind had gone.

"You sound like Hannah," he said with a laugh, "but if she were awake, she'd tell you I suck when it comes to fairy tales. I can't tell her a bedtime story without the CliffsNotes in front of me."

Rory laughed. "Don't worry. You already know this one. It's the origin story of a successful lawyer with a hidden background as a blue-collar construction worker."

"Not hidden," Jamison argued, feeling his face heat at the lie.

"So this is something you do a lot?" she pressed. "Help friends with projects or volunteer with Habitat for Humanity?"

The simplest thing would have been to agree and hope Rory would leave it at that. But from the moment they met, she'd challenged him not to take the easy way out. Not when it came to Hannah and not when it came to telling the truth about himself. "I haven't picked up a hammer in almost a decade," he confessed.

"But once upon a time..."

A gruff laugh escaped him at the teasing look in her eyes. "Once upon a time," he began, "I worked construction while I was in college. That's how Ryder and I met."

"So you weren't—" Rory cut herself off, but Jamison had a feeling where her thoughts had gone.

"Born with a silver spoon in my mouth?" He shook his head, hardly offended by the assumption when he spent most of his life trying to give that very impression. "Not even close. My parents had me when they were barely out of their teens. Neither one of them took more than a few college courses. My mom worked as a receptionist off and on, and my dad was a handyman, taking on whatever jobs he could find."

"And he's the one who taught you how to do this," Rory said, waving a hand at the gazebo with an expression of pride that sent guilt stabbing through Jamison's heart.

"Yeah, my dad taught me a lot of things." And Jamison had repaid him by being ashamed and spending most of the past fifteen years pretending the man didn't exist.

"But the things my dad could do… It was never enough for my mother. They fought all the time. Over everything, it seemed, but mostly over money. My mom was the one who always encouraged me to do more, to be better, to—"

Do whatever you have to do so you don't end up spending your life cleaning toilets like your father.

Jamison shook his head, trying to dislodge his mother's bitter words from his memory. "Anyway, when I was ten or so, she got it in her head that public school wasn't good enough and that I needed to go to prep school."

"Prep school? As in matching uniforms with jackets and ties and argyle socks?"

He gave a mock shudder. "It was that bad and worse."

"Hard to imagine worse."

"Worse was knowing I didn't belong in that uniform. That I was the charity case—the kid who could only afford to go to Winston Prep because my dad took a job there as a janitor and my tuition was waived.

"My mother was the one who was so determined I go to that school, and my dad made it happen the only way he could. But that wasn't good enough for her, either. She hated that he worked there, was always putting him down, and after a while, I started to feel the same way. I didn't want the other kids knowing he was my dad."

"It's hard to think of anyone other than yourself when you're a kid."

"When they divorced my freshman year, I thought the constant fighting would be over. But in some ways it got worse. Like they no longer had to even pretend that they cared about each other. I got caught in the middle and felt like I had to make a choice, and I chose to stay with my mom.

"After so many years of hearing how we deserved better and how I had it in me to 'be something' so long as I didn't let my dad bring me down... I don't know. I guess I started to buy into it. I wanted the expensive shoes and the latest electronics and the fancy cars like everyone else at Winston had, and when my mom remarried that first time, to a rich guy she met thanks to her making friends with the parents of kids who went to Winston, I got all that stuff."

"The first time your mother remarried?"

"First, but not last. She's on her fourth marriage. Fifth, I guess, if you count that she married number three twice."

"Ouch."

"It's made Father's Day interesting."

"I'm sorry, Jamison."

"Don't be. I made my choice. I could have gone to live with my dad, but I liked have*ing* all those shoes and toys and cars." Jamison shook his head. "You know, even after my mom remarried, and my stepdad was footing all the bills and could afford to pay my tuition a thousand times over, my dad kept working at that school. A thankless, low-paying job he must have hated...just so he could still see me."

"I'm guessing that made it all worth it for him."

"I wish I'd appreciated all he was willing to do for me and that I hadn't cut him out of my life the way I did."

"But that was then. What about now?"

"It's been better...especially over the past few years.

Mostly thanks to Hannah." A smile touched his face as he said his daughter's name. "I reached out to him after she was born, and he's made a real effort to get to know her, to be there for birthdays and holidays. He enjoys being a grandfather."

"I'm glad…for Hannah, but also for you and your father."

"Yeah, me, too," Jamison agreed, but he couldn't help thinking of the years he'd lost—both with his father and with Hannah.

Two of the most important people in his life, and he'd failed them both. First as a son and then as a father.

As much as he'd enjoyed the past few days and as familiar as a hammer felt in his hand, Jamison couldn't see giving up everything he'd worked for—the struggle to put himself through college, the countless hours of studying to get through law school, the prestige of working at Spears, Moreland and Howe, and the promise of the partnership— even if it would be best for Hannah.

His dad had made that kind of sacrifice, but Jamison couldn't help feeling he was very much his mother's son. He loved his daughter, he did, but Jamison couldn't help feeling something lacking inside him kept him from loving her *enough*.

Chapter Nine

The first annual Clearville Cowboy Days was in full swing by the time the sun started sinking behind the horizon, painting the sky with a pinkish-orange hue. Warm summer air carried the sound of laughter and, as long as the wind wasn't coming from the arena, the mouthwatering scent of smoky barbecue. Along with the draw of the rodeo, walkways led toward a fenced-off petting zoo and a carnival-style midway lined with cheesy stuffed-animal prizes. Bells and whistles rang out mixed with groans and cheers from the spectators gathered around the games.

"I still can't believe this turnout."

"Yeah, it's impressive," Jamison responded, trying to match his friend's enthusiasm as he, Ryder and Lindsay dodged the boisterous crowds checking out the Rockin' R benefit rodeo.

"The chamber of commerce has worked with Jarrett Deeks and his wife, Theresa, on the event," Lindsay chimed in. "The hope is to raise money and awareness for their horse rescue, but it's also a chance for Clearville to shine."

"A chance for you to shine," Ryder told his fiancée with a proud smile that had Lindsay shaking her head.

"Theresa and Jarrett already had much of this in place before I moved back and came on board. They're the ones who deserve credit."

"Says the woman who's been working tirelessly on promotion and sponsorship and vendors—"

"All right, all right! I'll take some credit if it'll make you hush up!"

"I bet you can think of better ways to shut me up," Ryder challenged with a suggestive lift to his eyebrows.

"You do realize other people can hear you, right?" Jamison's pointed comment had his friend grinning even more unrepentantly while Lindsay gave his shoulder a quick shove.

"You're crazy, you know that?"

"Only about you."

At that, Lindsay showed she did indeed know how to shut Ryder up as she rose onto her tiptoes to keep his mouth occupied with a kiss.

Jamison jerked his gaze away to focus on a trio of dusty cowboys, complete with hats, chaps and bandannas, laughing with a group of wide-eyed, flirty girls, none of whom looked old enough for all the makeup they were wearing, let alone the beers they were drinking.

All in all, Jamison felt as out of place as…well, a corporate lawyer at a rodeo.

But it wasn't the retro Wild West setting that had him feeling so uncomfortable. It was playing third wheel to Ryder and Lindsay, an unnecessary cog to the obvious affection and attraction between them.

"Are you sure the kids are okay going off by themselves?"

"They're fine, Dad," Ryder teased.

Lindsay's response was more sympathetic. "I know Robbie, Tyler and Brayden are still young," she said, referring to her son and his two cousins, "but they're good boys. They'll keep an eye on Hannah, and the carnival games are all being run by locals who'll watch out for them, too."

"Yeah, I'm sure you're right."

He'd worried about Hannah's reaction to the loud noises, huge animals and large crowd, but his concerns had been misplaced. After little more than a brief hesitation, Hannah had taken off with the boys, leaving Jamison feeling... bereft. Suddenly, he was the one feeling out of place and overwhelmed.

They'd spent so much time together the past few days, he missed having his daughter at his side...as much as he found himself missing Rory.

He still didn't know why he'd agreed to go to the rodeo—other than the thought that Rory might be there. And if that wasn't the stupidest move ever, he didn't know what was. Going to the rodeo on the off chance of catching a glimpse of the beautiful brunette when he could have gone *with* her.

She'd issued the invitation as she'd packed up their picnic lunch the day before. "From what Lindsay says, they'll have all kinds of music, food and even games planned for the kids. Anyway, I was wondering if you and Hannah would like to go. You know—" she rolled her eyes, a hint of color brightening her cheeks "—with me?"

Jamison had swallowed the instant agreement that came to mind. "Rory... I'm leaving in just over a week."

"I know," she'd shot back quickly, her eyes and smile still bright. "But fortunately for us, the rodeo is tomorrow. You're still here tomorrow."

He should have expected she wouldn't give up easily,

not a woman who'd been willing to fight for a man she thought was *the one*. But like the ex who had let her down, Jamison knew he'd done the same.

The disappointment in her gaze should have been enough to make him keep his distance. Rory wasn't the type of woman to have a summer fling, and he couldn't offer her anything more. He'd be going back to a life that already felt overbooked with the pressure of the upcoming promotion and the responsibility of raising Hannah on his own.

"Lookie, Daddy, Tyler won me a fuzzy unicorn!" Hannah's voice broke into his thoughts as she raced toward him, and Jamison wondered what it said about him that he was as eager to see his daughter as she was to see him.

"He did, huh?" Jamison bent down to examine the purple-and-white stuffed animal she proudly held out.

"Uh-huh! For me!" His daughter nodded, her ponytail bobbing exuberantly. She didn't seem to care that the poor thing was slightly cross-eyed, its golden horn already bent, as she gazed at the older boy with a look of pure hero worship.

The brown-haired boy trailing behind her with his younger brother and Robbie scuffed his oversize tennis shoe against the loose gravel. "No big deal. It was one of those dart games where you have to pop the balloons. The prizes were all lame—uh, kinda girlie."

Ryder smiled at his nephew's deflection of Hannah's praise. "Way to go making a little girl's night, dude."

Tyler ducked his head, but he still held up his hand for his uncle's high five.

"I think someone might have a little crush," Lindsay teased, and Jamison didn't know which of them was more horrified—ten-year-old Tyler or his thirty-one-year-old self.

Just the thought of makeup, short skirts and puberty

had panic racing through him, and he longed to hold on to the unicorn and hope for a miracle that would keep his daughter a little girl forever.

"Hey, Dad, can we have some money to go get something to eat?"

As Ryder handed the boys some cash, Lindsay warned, "Not too much junk food."

"Yeah, right," Ryder snorted as the boys took off, jostling each other as they went. "I'm sure they're heading straight for the booth selling the organic quinoa."

A few yards away, Robbie turned back. "Hannah, you wanna come?"

"Can I, Daddy?" She looked up at him, her eyes filled with happiness and hope, and something caught inside his chest.

"Yeah," he said, his voice husky. "Go have fun."

She turned to race after the boys before circling back. "Here." She thrust the unicorn into his arms. "You can hold Uni. He'll keep you comp'ny."

Bending down to her level, he tapped the mythical creature's bent horn against her forehead. "Thanks, Hannah Banana."

She giggled at the nickname and threw her arms around him in a quick hug that had Jamison swallowing against the sudden lump in his throat.

Rory might not have been by his side, but she was there. He could feel her presence in Hannah's smile. She'd given his little girl back her laughter, her sense of adventure, her willingness to try…and he wondered at what might be possible if only he was half as brave as his daughter.

"Come on!"

Rory stumbled, trying to keep up with Debbie Pirelli as her friend dragged her through the Clearville fairgrounds toward the sound of country-western music. Boots might have been the right fashion choice, but they weren't the most comfortable. She slipped more than once on the fairground's loose gravel before they reached the stage. A local band had taken their place in the spotlight, and a dozen or so wannabe cowboys were boot scooting their ladies across a makeshift dance floor.

"I'm not sure this is a good idea," Rory protested.

"Trust me! This will be fun!"

Following at a slower pace a yard or so behind, Drew Pirelli laughed. "I can't tell you how many things she's talked me into with those same words!"

The vivacious blonde sent her husband a grin over her shoulder. "Like you're complaining!"

"Um, he might not be," Rory said after Drew offered to stand in line for drinks at the nearby booth, "but did I mention I'm not a fan of country music?"

Her friend laughed again. "You do know this is a rodeo, right? I don't think they'll be playing too much classical music around here tonight!"

Debbie was Hillcrest's exclusive wedding cake designer, and Rory had gotten to know the talented baker and café owner over the past few months. She'd been surprised and pleased when Debbie had called to see if she wanted to go to the rodeo. The last thing she wanted was for her new friend to think she wasn't enjoying her company. "Thanks again for inviting me. I'd been looking forward to this night, but I wouldn't have come by myself."

"Ah, now I get it," Debbie said as she bounced on her toes in time with the music.

"Get what?"

"You wanted to come with someone else."

"No, I—not really," she mumbled. She'd hoped to go with Jamison and Hannah. Rory loved seeing the little girl come out of her shell, how her first few steps in trying something new were always a little hesitant, but once she found her footing, she was ready to hit the ground running.

And Jamison…he was running, too. Only he was running away.

"I can't figure him out," she muttered, not realizing she'd spoken the words out loud until Debbie jumped on them.

"Who?"

"What?"

"Who is this mystery man we're talking about? The one you can't figure out but would like to be two-stepping across the dance floor with right now."

That was enough to startle a snort right out her. "Two-stepping is the last thing I can picture Jamison…"

Rory swallowed a curse as Debbie crowed with laughter. "I knew it! I knew there was some guy you'd rather be with right now." Her eyes widened further. "Wait… Jamison. Isn't that the single dad who's been bringing his adorable daughter into the café for cookies this week? No wonder you're not into cowboys if a guy like that is your type."

"That's part of the problem. Jamison is the exact opposite of my type."

Debbie raised a knowing eyebrow. "Funny. That's what I said about Drew. Once upon a time."

Ignoring her friend's words, Rory said, "He can be so serious, so logical, so lawyery…" And he probably would have been the first to call her on making up words, had he been there.

"Not to mention seriously sexy, practically gorgeous—"

"Okay, stop. I don't need to hear all of that. Especially not after making a fool out of myself over him yesterday."

"Ooh, that sounds promising." Debbie's blue eyes lit up with curiosity. "Give me the gory details."

Rory might have made it seem like Debbie was pulling the information out of her, but deep down, she needed someone to talk to. No way could she go to Evie when her cousin's line between business and pleasure was more like the Great Wall. And Rory didn't feel comfortable talking to Lindsay about her fiancé's best friend.

She was careful, though, not to reveal too much of Jamison's past. He'd opened up to her in a way she doubted he did with too many people, and she would hold fast to what he'd told her in confidence.

"I know this attraction between us isn't meant to last, that he'll be going back to San Francisco after the wedding." And if she wasn't careful, she'd be heartbroken when he left her behind. "Maybe he's right. Why bother to start something that's destined to come to an end?"

Debbie glanced past Rory and her grin widened even further. "We need to find you a dance partner."

Thrown by the abrupt change in topic, Rory said, "I'm not sure how that's going to help."

"Oh, believe me, it will. Jamison thinks he's being all noble by keeping his distance, but that's sure to fade fast when he sees you in the arms of another guy."

"Sees me?" Rory's heart skipped a beat even before she glanced over her shoulder to what had captured Debbie's attention a few seconds earlier. Or more specifically who…

Jamison stood outside the crowd gathered near the beer garden. His chestnut hair gleamed even in the artificial light. He wore a black T-shirt and jeans, perhaps in an effort to fit in, but for Rory, he still stood out. He was more masculine, more striking than the men around him, and that was even with the stuffed unicorn he held in one long-fingered hand.

She jerked her attention back up to find her gaze snagged on his lips and the memory of his kiss. Thirty feet and two dozen or so people separated them, but the distance, the crowd, the music, all of it faded away until only the two of them existed. Right up until the moment he turned away...

"Dance," Debbie commanded and just like that, the rest of the world rushed back in. Only it was too close, too crowded, too noisy.

"I don't feel like dancing," she protested weakly as she lost sight of Jamison in the line of people milling around the drink booths.

Debbie shook her head. "This isn't about how you feel. This is about making Jamison face how *he* feels."

"I don't even see him anymore. He's probably not even paying attention."

"Oh, trust me, he's still watching." Her friend grinned "And it's up to you to make sure there's something to see."

He couldn't stop watching. Try as he might to pull his gaze from the crowded dance floor, to stop staring at Rory like some kind of stalker, his attention returned to her time and again. In the brief seconds when he would lose sight of her during the turns and twists of complicated line dances he couldn't begin to follow, his heart would stop...only to start racing double time when he once again caught a flash of her ruffled denim skirt or the red bandanna material of her sleeveless top.

She was far from the best dancer on the floor. She'd stumbled once or twice, turned the wrong way and even bumped into a dancer next to her. But through it all, she kept smiling, laughing despite her embarrassment, her blue eyes sparkling and her dark ponytail swaying in time with the music.

"Here you go," Ryder said as he handed Jamison the chilled bottle of beer that had brought them over to the area by the dance floor in the first place. "Sorry it took so long. Man, those lines are crazy."

The brew was cold and crisp but did little to douse the fire in his gut as the music changed, switching from a boot-scooting beat to the slow, mellow strains of a waltz. Like some kind of switch had been flipped, the crowd of people who'd been standing side by side started pairing off, leaving Rory alone. But only for a moment...

A split second in time when her gaze met his, the pull strong enough he caught his body swaying in her direction.

I'm leaving soon.

His reasoning for keeping his distance hadn't changed, but neither did Rory's response. He didn't need to hear the words to read what was written in her expression.

You're here now.

A blond cowboy stepped between them, blocking Rory from his sight. The other guy was tall and wide enough that Jamison couldn't see Rory's answer to the question the cowboy asked, but a second later, her slender hand curved over the guy's broad shoulder as he took her into his arms.

Dragging his gaze away with a curse, Jamison sucked in a lungful of air, suddenly realizing he'd forgotten how to breathe in the last few moments. He needed to get out of there before he made the best worst mistake of his life. "I need to check on Hannah," he said, but Ryder was shaking his head.

"Lindsay's already talked to Robbie. They're having a great time. They've left the food court and are heading over to the kiddie rides."

"Maybe I should go—"

"She's fine, man. She doesn't need you to hold her hand...but maybe you need her to hold yours?"

"What the hell is that supposed to mean?"

"Just that strangling that unicorn isn't helping your mood any. Maybe you think having Hannah around will keep your mind off a certain wedding coordinator strutting her stuff out on the dance floor."

"I'm not—she's—" Cutting himself off, Jamison set the stuffed animal he'd forgotten he was still holding on a nearby table and took another long pull of the beer he no longer wanted. "Rory's free to dance with whomever she wants."

"Yeah, right," Ryder gave a doubting scoff, and Jamison couldn't blame his friend. Even the cross-eyed unicorn seemed to be gazing at him disbelief, but it was the truth…

"Go ask her. Unless you're afraid she'll say no."

He was afraid she'd say yes. Rory might have been in the arms of another man, but it didn't matter whom she danced with or how many times.

That could have been me.

It *should* have been him.

"Hannah! Oh, sweetie, what happened?"

Lindsay's cry jerked his attention from the dance floor in time to see three guilty-looking boys leading a sniffling Hannah their way. Tyler and Robbie exchanged a quick glance before Tyler said, "She, um, kinda got sick after we went on the merry-go-round."

"Yeah," the youngest boy chimed in, "it was super gross and—"

"Brayden, dude."

"Oh, right." The boy ducked his head at his uncle's reproach and mumbled, "We're real sorry she got sick."

"Daddy, I don't feel so good." A flood of tears balanced on Hannah's lower lids, and Jamison froze.

The sight of his daughter's tears instantly sent him back to those first horrible days after the accident when all

Hannah could do was cry for her mother and there'd been nothing—*nothing*—Jamison could do to soothe her fears.

Lindsay reached out to smooth Hannah's hair back from her sweaty forehead in the way all mothers seemed to know how to do. "Poor thing. They have a first-aid station set up near the front entrance—"

Alarmed, Jamison broke out of his paralysis. "You think she's that sick?" Knowing Hannah's fear of hospitals—the place where her mother had died—he didn't want to traumatize her further unless a trip to the doctor was absolutely necessary.

"No, not at all. I think she had too much junk food combined with too much excitement, but they can help clean her up and maybe give her something to settle her stomach."

Bending down, he tried to keep his own stomach from roiling as he took in the bluish-purple mess staining the front of his daughter's T-shirt. What on earth had she eaten that would be that color coming back up? "What do you think, Hannah? Do you want to go get cleaned up and see what we can do to make you feel better?"

But Hannah shook her head, her lower lip protruding in a trembling pout. "No." She wobbled. "I want—I want m—"

Jamison braced himself only to be blown away by a request he never saw coming. "I want Miss Rory."

Chapter Ten

Her heart still in her throat, Rory ducked into the first-aid tent. She barely took in the small space with its two empty cots and a rolling cart stacked with bandages, gauze and bottles of peroxide and iodine before her gaze locked on the third occupied bed.

"Miss Rory..." Hannah's brown eyes filled and her lower lip trembled as she spotted her. "I got sick."

"I know, sweetie. I heard, and I'm so sorry you don't feel good." Hazarding a glance at Jamison, standing like a sentinel near the foot of his daughter's bed, Rory added, "Your daddy called me and said you wanted me to come see you."

She'd heard the reluctance in his voice as he explained how the little girl had gotten sick and that he'd taken her to the first-aid area. How he hadn't wanted to bother her...

But Rory had the feeling Jamison was the one who was bothered—by Hannah needing her. And maybe, just maybe, by how he needed her, too...

The little girl nodded, giving a watery sniff and wiping at a tear with the back of her hand. She was wearing one of the Rockin' R souvenir T-shirts. The oversize sleeves hung down to her elbows, making her look even smaller and more vulnerable.

As soon as Rory sat down on the cot, Hannah climbed onto her lap…and right into her heart. Closing her eyes against the undeniable realization, she breathed in the sweet scent of baby shampoo combined with mint toothpaste. Little more than a week, and Rory had fallen hard, and she didn't dare think about her feelings for the sad-eyed girl's father…

"I'm feeling better now," she mumbled into Rory's shoulder.

"Don't count on it."

At Jamison's dry comment, Rory couldn't help but glance up at him. He too looked a little pale and green around the gills, and she finally noticed Hannah wasn't the only one wearing a brand-new souvenir T-shirt.

She pressed her lips together to keep from laughing, but judging by the way he shook his head, she didn't succeed in hiding her amusement. "So glad you—and everyone—find this so funny."

"I don't think it's funny, Daddy." Hannah wrinkled her nose in an exaggerated expression of disgust. "I think it was yucky."

"And that," a female voice chimed in, "is what we in the nursing field would call a spot-on diagnosis."

Rory looked up as Theresa Deeks handed Jamison a plastic bag containing Hannah and Jamison's damp shirt. She hadn't realized the pretty nurse would be overseeing the first-aid station, though Theresa was certain to be on hand after all the work she and her husband, Jarrett, had put into making the rodeo such a success.

"I rinsed them out, but they'll still need a good washing."

"That wasn't necessary."

The dark-haired woman laughed. "It was if either of you hoped to wear them again."

"That's my favorite shirt," Hannah chimed in, her voice forlorn.

Jamison looked slightly exasperated by his daughter's "woe is me" sigh but merely said, "Then I thank you for saving my daughter's favorite shirt."

"You're welcome, and as long as Hannah is feeling up to it, you can take her home."

"Come on, kiddo." Jamison reached out, but the little girl burrowed deeper into Rory's arms.

"I want Miss Rory."

"Hannah—"

"It's okay, Jamison. I'll ride back to the hotel with the two of you."

"Are you sure?"

At her nod, he leaned down to reach for Hannah. The move brought Rory and Jamison face-to-face, and even with his daughter between them, her breath caught at his nearness. Nerves danced in her stomach as if she'd been the one to have way too much junk food.

Jamison stood, lifting his daughter from her lap, and Rory was surprised at how empty her arms felt. Picking up the unicorn that had been tucked against Hannah's side, she was glad to have something to hold on to. Something to occupy her hands and to stop her from reaching out to smooth the oversize shirt over Hannah's back...or to try to ease the frown from Jamison's forehead.

"This is my fault. I should have been paying closer attention to Hannah and not—"

Watching you.

He didn't say the words, but Rory still heard them, and

even though he was blaming himself, she couldn't help feeling like he felt she, too, was somehow at fault. She'd taken more than her fair share of blame when she'd done nothing wrong, and this was one time where she wasn't going to keep quiet.

"Mrs. Deeks…"

"You can call me Theresa," the dark-haired woman offered over her shoulder as she wheeled the cart out of the way.

"Theresa, is Hannah the only child to come in with a bellyache tonight?"

"Are you kidding? We've had half a dozen or so little kids come through already. And don't even get me started on the big kids," she added as she crossed her arms over her chest. Offering a sympathetic smile, she told Jamison, "Your daughter's going to be fine. In a little while, you can try to get her to drink some flat soda to keep hydrated and crackers or dry toast if she's hungry. By morning, I'm betting she'll be back to her old self."

Jamison didn't say much once they left the first-aid tent and headed for his SUV. He strapped Hannah into her car seat, tucking her stuffed unicorn in next to her, and had pulled out of the parking lot before he glanced Rory's way.

The fairgrounds were located outside town, connected by a two-lane highway lined with towering pines but not the typical streetlights. Without the passing glow, the interior of the car was too dark for Rory to read his expression.

Hannah drifted off to sleep, and Rory might have found the soft sound of her breathing soothing if not for the tension she sensed coming off Jamison in waves.

Was he still blaming himself for Hannah getting sick? For not paying more attention to how much junk food one little girl could eat in a very short time span? They were almost back at the hotel when he spoke.

"I'm sorry. I'm sure this isn't what you had in mind for how tonight would end."

"And what do you think I had in mind?"

"I saw you earlier. Dancing. Having fun."

She must have been a better actress than she gave herself credit for if Jamison had thought she was enjoying herself. She'd tried. She had, appreciating the effort Drew and Debbie had put into including her.

But that hadn't stopped her from wishing Jamison had been on the dance floor beside her, that he had been the man to pull her into his arms and hold her body close as they swayed in time with the music.

And when her phone rang and his name lit up the screen—

"Actually, this is exactly how I hoped tonight would end."

She didn't need passing streetlights to recognize the incredulous look he shot her. "Leaving early with a sick kid?"

"With the three of us spending time together."

"Rory." Jamison made a sound that was half laugh, half groan. "I'm trying to do the right thing here."

"And if we disagree on what the right thing is? Then what?"

"We're leaving in just over a week. If we start something—if we—then what?"

She knew the answer as well as he did and couldn't deny the ache in her heart at the thought of saying goodbye. But worrying about the future wouldn't stop it from coming. All they could do was make the most of the time they did have. As far as she was concerned, that was the only right thing to do.

"If you left tomorrow, I wouldn't miss you any less."

Rory heard his quick intake of breath, but he didn't reply as he pulled into the Hillcrest House parking lot and cut the engine. The golden glow from the safety lights bathed the SUV's interior, and she could see what she'd missed before. The muscle working in his jaw, the tendons standing out in stark relief along his forearms, his hands tight on the steering wheel as if they were flying down the freeway. Holding himself back when every fiber in her being ached for him to hold her...

Deciding to put her cards on the table, Rory shifted on the passenger seat to face him. "I adore your little girl, Jamison, and I—I like you."

His hands clenched around the wheel tight enough that the leather squeaked beneath his grip.

"I know that makes me sound like a twelve-year-old with a foolish crush—"

Now he responded, quickly cutting off her words. "I think you're smart and brave and amazing. Which is why I can't do this."

"Do what?"

"Pretend to be the kind of man you deserve. A good father...a good husband...a good son... Name any kind of relationship, and it's one I've already failed. I don't know what this is between us, but I don't want it to be—I don't want *you* to be one more person I fail."

Debbie was right, Rory realized. He really did think he was being noble by keeping his distance. She might have admired his effort if she wasn't so tempted to smack him upside the head.

"You only fail when you stop trying. You haven't stopped trying with your father and you won't stop trying with Hannah. Not because that's the kind of man I deserve, but because that's the kind of man you are. And as for the two of us..." She sucked in a deep breath of her own. "I know how this ends, Jamison. With you and Hannah saying goodbye. Whether we spend those days together or not, that doesn't change. Whether you kiss me right now or not, that doesn't change. So the only question is…why not kiss me?"

Why not kiss me?

The words, the temptation, pounded through Jamison's veins in time with the blood beating from his heart. At the moment, he wasn't sure which was more vital. His heart had maintained the steady rhythm for the past thirty-one years, but he'd never felt this…aware. This alive.

Fortunately—or unfortunately, damned if he knew which—he hadn't had a chance to answer Rory's question. With the motion of the vehicle no longer lulling her into sleep, Hannah woke up and he'd lifted his sleepy, grumpy daughter against his chest. She held on tight to her new toy and the stuffed unicorn rode along his shoulder as she wrapped her arms around his neck.

The warm weight of her in his arms, combined with the trust and faith she placed in him, brought an ache to his throat. He pressed a kiss to her tangled curls as he breathed in her baby shampoo scent. Rory was right. He wasn't quitting on his little girl. He didn't know how he'd manage being a full-time single dad and a full-time lawyer, but he'd find a way.

Even though it wasn't very late, the hotel lobby was quiet—most of the guests were either at the rodeo or out enjoying dinner. Even so, Jamison was conspicuously aware of Rory walking by his side toward the Bluebell suite.

They needed to talk, to finish the conversation they'd started in the car but—

Why not kiss me?

Jamison sucked in a breath as they turned down the narrow hallway. He was going to have one hell of a time focusing on talking when he had Rory alone in a hotel room.

He carried Hannah straight into the suite's connecting bathroom and, within minutes, had her surrounded by a tub full of bubbles. Rory joined them a few seconds later, making the small space positively claustrophobic as she placed a hand on his shoulder and set a pair of pajamas on the toilet seat.

"Can you, um, hand me that washcloth?" The folded cloth at the edge of the tub wasn't so far that he couldn't have reached it, but Jamison found himself wanting Rory to stay. As she knelt by his side, helping Hannah hold the washcloth against her face as he rinsed the warm, sudsy water from her hair, it hit him this was the first time he'd ever shared Hannah's bath-time duties.

Before their separation, Monica—or, he later suspected, the nanny the Stiltons hired to "help out" their daughter— had been responsible. Now the nighttime duty was his alone.

I won't miss you any less if you left tomorrow.

God, wasn't that the truth, he thought as Rory wrapped his daughter in an oversize towel, drawing out a sleepy smile. Within minutes, she had Hannah dressed and still giggling from her first attempt to put the little girl's pajama top on inside out and backward.

But once Jamison tucked his daughter into bed and Rory kissed her good-night, Hannah hugged her unicorn to her chest, huge tears filling her brown eyes.

"Oh, Hannah, do you still feel yucky?"

Nodding her head vehemently, Hannah gave a watery sniff. Then, with a single blink, the dam burst. Silent tears coursed down her chubby cheeks.

"Sweetie…"

As Rory sank down on the bed beside her, the little girl threw her arms around her neck. "Can you sleep in my bed tonight?"

"Hannah," Jamison started but he could already see

Rory melting like Hannah's cotton candy at the first splash of water. He didn't doubt his daughter wasn't feeling well. He had a souvenir T-shirt and a possible lifelong aversion to brightly colored spun sugar to prove it.

But that didn't mean Hannah wasn't playing on the grown-ups' sympathy and using tears to get her way. After all his years with Monica, he'd built up a slight tolerance. Rory had no such immunity.

"Of course, Hannah." Curling up on her side next to the little girl, she promised, "I'll stay right here until you fall asleep."

Having done their trick, Hannah's tears performed a magical disappearing act as she snuggled beneath the covers.

"Daddy, too."

Hannah patted the empty spot on the other side of the bed, and Rory's eyes flew wide. The startled look and instant color heating her cheeks were reminders that she wasn't as bold as her words.

He knew he should play this smart and keep his distance. Starting something determined to end in such a short time made no sense in his logical, well-ordered world. But then again, he'd never met anyone like Rory McClaren in his logical, well-ordered world.

A little over a week ago, he wouldn't have believed such a charming, magical woman existed. And the chance to spend eight days—hell, even another eight minutes—with her would make spending the rest of his life missing her a price he was willing to pay.

The last thing Rory expected when she closed her eyes and pretended to sleep was to drift off. But as she lay on the bed with Hannah curled up against her side, keeping her breathing slow and steady—thinking that might encourage her rapidly beating heart to do the same—trying to lull the little girl into a peaceful slumber, she somehow followed right along.

She woke slowly, taking in the unfamiliar warmth pressed against her side and something soft and furry brushing her face. She blinked as she waited for her eyes to adjust to the dim light shining in from the doorway. Brushing the unicorn's fluffy tail aside, Rory smiled at the sight of Hannah's angelic features, sweet and soft in sleep. She looked over the little girl's blond head to Jamison's handsome face. Not sweet, not soft.

Not asleep.

Her mouth went dry as she met his glittering gaze. "Um, what time is it?" The question wasn't the one she wanted to give voice to, but she couldn't quite bring herself to ask how long he'd been watching her sleep.

She was tempted to pull the blanket over her head as the humiliation of another question she shouldn't have asked throbbed in the stillness of the night. She might as well have begged him to kiss her, and that was after he'd already turned her down once!

"Late…or early, depending on how you look at it."

"I should go." Sliding out of the bed, she placed the stuffed animal under Hannah's arm and smoothed out the blankets, wishing she could smooth her rattled nerves as easily.

Focused on getting Hannah ready for bed, Rory had pushed the final minutes of their conversation out of her mind. But now the words pinballed through her skull, pained embarrassment flashing all around. She'd thought the way Jamison had kissed her, the way they'd opened up to each other, sharing hurts and fears from their pasts, had meant something.

But she'd been wrong before.

Ducking out of the bedroom, Rory hurried down the

shadowed hallway as fast as her boots could carry her. She'd keep her attention where it should have been all along, on Ryder and Lindsay's wedding, on getting through the next week, and then she could forget all about Jamison, all about Hannah, all about how her heart was breaking inside her chest...

She'd barely made it to the living room when Jamison caught her by the shoulders, stopping her short and drawing her back against him. His warm breath stirred her hair and sent shivers running down her spine as he murmured in her ear. "If you leave now, I won't miss you any less."

For a split second, she allowed herself lean into the warmth and strength of his body before growing a backbone and pulling away. He let her go, and Rory spun to face him, ready to remind him he didn't want this, didn't want *her*, but the sheer longing in his expression sucked the words right from her chest.

"Jamison—" The whispered sound of his name hovered in the charged air between them. A connection drawing them closer as he reached up to cup her face in his hands.

His thumbs caressed her cheeks, her lips, charting a sensual path that held her captivated. Her heart pounded, running a hundred beats a minute, but she couldn't even move. "Jamison—"

Light as a feather, his lips moved against hers as he spoke. Her stunned senses barely recognized the words. "So why not kiss me?"

Rory didn't know what it was about this man that was magic, but one kiss and she'd swear she could fly. She fisted her hands in the crisp cotton of the Rockin' R T-shirt as if he might somehow keep her grounded, but how could he when it was his touch, his kiss that had her body, her heart, her soul soaring? And then her feet really did leave the earth as she sank onto the couch cushions, Jamison following her down, his body strong, warm, *perfect* above hers.

He deepened the kiss as her mouth opened to his—touching, tasting, teasing. His hand found the narrow gap between the bandanna-print shirt tied at her waist and the top of her skirt. Her skin sizzled at the contact, and it was all she could do not to arch her body into his, wanting, demanding, needing more—

But she could feel him holding back. Like a kite with a string still tethered to the ground, Rory could feel the tug of resistance, the slow, unrelenting pull reeling them back to earth as he broke the kiss.

This time she didn't let old insecurities get in the way, didn't doubt his desire for her. "Jamison," she whispered softly once she'd found the breath and ability to speak.

He dropped his forehead against her shoulder, his body rock hard as he fought for control. "We can't," he started as he lifted his head.

"I know," she smiled, his willingness to put his daughter first one of the reasons why she loved hm.

Loved him?

No! She couldn't—she didn't—she—

Loved him.

Rory slammed her eyes shut, too afraid of the emotions Jamison might see. "I should go."

The cushions shifted beneath her as he pushed into a sitting position and lifted her up beside him. She felt as well as heard the words he spoke against her ear. "Rory... I wish—I want—"

"I know." Her heart was suddenly filled with wishes and wants, but closing her eyes wasn't going to be enough to make them come true. Lifting her lashes, she repeated, "I should go."

"As long as you know how much I want you to stay.

You were right before. I want us to spend the time we have left together."

Rory didn't know if she wanted to laugh or cry. She'd convinced Jamison—straitlaced, logical Jamison—to take a leap, and now she was the one who wanted to play things safe. To protect her heart, to take a step back from the edge rather than risk a nasty fall.

"Tell me you still want that, too, Rory," he urged, his hands bracketing her shoulders. "I'm here now, and I don't want to start missing you until I have to."

If you leave tomorrow...this won't hurt any less.

"I want that, too," she promised.

"Good." Pulling her back into his arms, he pressed a kiss to her temple. "Good."

Rory wasn't sure how long she stayed in his arms, her head resting on his chest as she counted out the beats of his heart. If only it didn't seem like the steady rhythm was going backward, counting down the time they had left…

It was still dark and Jamison was still sleeping when Rory eased out of his embrace and slipped out the door. The old-fashioned hallway sconces had been dimmed for the night, casting a soft golden glow on the familiar dark walnut wainscot and richly patterned carpet.

So overwhelmed by the emotions still careening through her, Rory barely noticed the two women she passed in the hallway until their sharp laughter stabbed her in the back.

"Guess those stories Trisha heard were right. She really can't keep her hands off the merchandise."

Chapter Eleven

Jamison jerked awake, startled by the unfamiliar ring of a telephone. Pain shot down his spine as he lifted his head, blinked a few times and realized he'd fallen asleep on the couch.

Rubbing the kink at the back of his neck, he pushed into a sitting position on the too-soft blue floral cushions. He hadn't planned to spend the night on the couch, but then again, much of what happened last night had been completely unexpected…

He took a quick look around to confirm what he already knew. Rory was gone. He didn't blame her for leaving. The last thing she would want was for someone to see her slipping out of a guest's room in the middle of the night.

That didn't mean he didn't wish she'd stayed. Call him selfish, but he'd had the pleasure of falling asleep with her in his arms. He wanted to know what it was like to wake up the same way.

Still, maybe she was calling to check on Hannah and see if she felt up to another batch of smiley-face oatmeal. Anticipation wiped away the last traces of sleep as he grabbed the hotel phone off the end table.

"Jamison, my boy! How are you doing up there in Smallville?"

He cringed at the sound of his former father-in-law's voice. Gregory Stilton was as big and imposing in person as his booming voice was over the phone. When Jamison first met Monica's father, he couldn't help being impressed by the businessman's wealth, status and importance. At the time, those things had still mattered to Jamison. Having just passed the bar and eager to make his mark, Jamison had seen Gregory Stilton as having it all.

"It's Clearville, Greg," he told the older man, "and everything's fine."

"Good, good. Glad to hear it. And how's our grand-daughter?"

His hand tightened around the phone. "She's doing fine."

His gaze locked on a piece of paper on the coffee table, a project Hannah had worked on the day before. It took some imagination, but even he recognized the lime-green grass, turquoise sky and silver gazebo. Three stick figures held hands in front of the structure. He might have wondered at his daughter's Picasso-like image of him if not for the big red smile filling up half his face.

"Better than fine," he added, hearing the pride in his voice. "She's doing great. She's looking forward to her role as a flower girl in Ryder's wedding."

"Well, that's great."

Over the years, Jamison had learned to distrust Greg's over-the-top friendliness. More often than not, he was hiding his own agenda behind his smile. He'd come to appreciate Louisa's open disdain. At least with his mother-in-law, he never had to guess where things stood.

Proving his suspicions correct, Greg casually commented, "Of course, this vacation of yours couldn't come at a worse time—what with the junior partnership up for grabs."

"How do you know about the partnership?"

Gregory's laughter ratcheted up Jamison's suspicion even more. "You're nearing the big time now, Jamison. The law firm of Spears, Moreland and Howe taking on a new partner is news. People have been taking about it at the club."

The firm's partners ran in a tight-knit circle of powerful men and women in San Francisco. It was possible Greg had heard the rumors. But it was also possible that, as a powerful man himself, Gregory Stilton would use his considerable influence to weigh in on which direction he wanted the firm to go.

"Greg…"

If the older man heard the warning in Jamison's tone, he ignored it. "You know if you get the promotion, you'll be spending even more time at the office—long hours, weekends. Have you thought about what you'll do with Hannah?"

"We've talked about this. She'll be starting preschool once I get back."

"Half days in the mornings," Greg pointed out dismissively. "And that's if you can get her to stay. You know how leery she is around strangers."

"Hannah's getting better about that."

Silence filled the other end of the line, and Jamison realized what he should have known all along when his mother-in-law's voice came across the speaker. "Getting better? What strangers have you been leaving her with up there?"

"Not strangers. What I meant is she's getting better about meeting new people." Knowing his in-laws would dig the information out of Hannah given the chance, he added, "Rory McClaren is the hotel's wedding coordinator, and Hannah's taken a shine to her. She's made the whole idea of being a flower girl fun for Hannah. That's a good thing, Louisa."

"Is it? I thought this trip was about you spending time with your daughter, not about finding someone else to watch her while you go off and—do whatever."

"I'm the best man. The only *whatever* I've been doing is lending a hand with the wedding, and I wasn't always able to do that without someone to help with Hannah."

Jamison heard Louisa mutter the words *party planner* and *responsible sitter* under her breath before Greg came back on the line. "We're glad our little girl's looking forward to the wedding. How about you put her on so we can both say hello?"

A loud yawn sounded from the bedroom doorway as Hannah shuffled out, rubbing one eye before she pushed some serious bed-head curls out of her face. "She's right here, but don't expect too much. She just woke up and might be a little cranky."

He held the phone away from his ear rather than listening to what Louisa thought of him letting his daughter sleep in late and past her scheduled breakfast time. "Hey, Hannah Banana, want to talk to Nana and Papa?"

Giving a sleepy nod, Hannah took the phone and scrambled onto the couch next to him. Some of the tension caused by speaking with his in-laws faded as she snuggled by his side. "Hi, Nana. Hi, Papa."

Jamison might have questioned if he'd done the right thing in bringing Rory up in a conversation with his in-laws, but his daughter proved he'd little choice as she launched into a recitation of everything she'd done over the past few days—with almost every sentence filled with "Rory this" or "Rory that."

And after his daughter capped off her story with a detailed account of throwing up the brightly colored cotton candy, Jamison figured Louisa was about ready to faint.

"I didn't feel good, so I wanted Miss Rory to spend the night. Daddy, where is Miss Rory?" Hannah frowned before thrusting the phone back at him. "Nana wants to talk to you."

I bet she does, Jamison thought grimly.

"What kind of example are you setting, having some strange woman spend the night—"

"She didn't spend the night, Louisa. She stayed until Hannah fell asleep."

No need for the woman to know what happened after Hannah fell asleep. Covering the mouthpiece, he told Hannah, "Rory had to go back to her house, but we'll see her in a little bit if you're feeling okay."

"I feel good, Daddy. But I don't think I should have cotton candy for breakfast."

"Wise decision, kiddo."

He'd barely paid attention to the final minutes of Louisa's tirade. He was sure he'd heard the lecture about strict schedules and maintaining routines a dozen times before. "It was one night of too much sugar and too much excitement," he finally interrupted. "She's fine now, Louisa. In fact, I'd say Hannah's happier than she's been in a long time."

I'm happier. And he refused to feel guilty about that even as a cold silence filled the other end of the line.

"And I suppose you think this Rory person has something to do with that."

"It's not about what *I* think, and if you were listening to anything your granddaughter had to say, you'd know that."

"My granddaughter is four, a child who can be easily manipulated and fooled. As her father, it's up to you to know better."

Jamison rolled his eyes. "No one's manipulating or fooling anyone."

"I guess we'll see about that."

"What does that mean?"

"It means I hope you know what you're doing," she told him before ending the call, the warning in her voice making it clear she didn't think he had a clue.

Jamison hopped down from the stepladder after putting the final touches of paint on the trim along the gazebo's roof and tossed the paintbrush into an empty bucket. "What do you think?"

"It's be-yoo-tiful, Daddy!"

Rory couldn't agree more. The gazebo gleamed against the bright blue midday sky as it never had before, shining like new and yet still maintaining all the old-world charm and romance that made it a perfect part of Hillcrest. She loved the elegant scrollwork along the eaves, a more delicate pattern than what had been there before. Jamison had found matching spindles to replace the loose railing, making the stairs as good as new.

But it was the special touch he'd added, one no one else could see, that meant the most. Beneath the top step, on the underside of the tread, Jamison had carved all their initials.

He hadn't inscribed them within a heart, but he didn't need to. He and Hannah had already etched a permanent spot within her own.

He smiled when he got a good look at his daughter's

face. "Hannah Banana, I think you have more paint on you than on the gazebo."

Their roles as helpers had involved touch-up work, painting over screw and nail heads with Hannah doing her best and Rory following behind to fix any missed areas and clean up any drips.

"Uh-uh!" the little girl argued before wrinkling her paint-splattered nose and turning to Rory. "Do I, Miss Rory?"

"Well, maybe not that much." Dipping the tip of her finger in an open paint can, Rory said, "But you do have some here…and here…and here."

Hannah giggled as Rory tapped her nose, cheeks and chin. "Now look, Daddy!"

Shaking his head with the slightest bit of exasperation, Jamison said, "Nice polka dots, kiddo."

"I like poky dots."

"Well, you can't have poky dots if we're going to go into town for something to eat, so we better get cleaned up."

"Yeah, pizza!"

"With lots of anchovies, right?" Rory teased as she grabbed a semiclean cloth and a bottle of water off the top of a cooler.

The little girl made a face. "Anchovies, yuck!"

"Hannah, you don't even know what anchovies are," Jamison pointed out.

"Are they good?" his daughter demanded, her doubt obvious.

"Well, no," he admitted, clearly failing to prove his point.

Hannah turned back to Rory in triumph. "No anchovies!"

"All right. How about—" Rory paused for a moment to think "—pepperoni?"

"Okay!" With the promise of pizza in the air, Hannah

bounced on her toes, making Rory's efforts to clean off her face like a new version of pin the tail on the donkey. "No anchovies, just pepperoni."

Once Rory had Hannah's face as clean as she could get it without a tub full of bubbles, she cupped her cute cheeks in her hands. "There you go. All clean."

Hannah responded with a definitive nod. "Daddy's turn."

Jamison had dropped down to sit on one of the stepladder's lower rungs, and when he brushed a hand across his damp forehead, he left behind a streak of white.

"Hannah is right." Lips quirked in a smile, she told him, "You're wearing almost as much paint as she was."

He took in his white-flecked shirt with a careless shrug as he cracked open the water bottle she handed him. "What can I say? Construction work is an ugly process."

Ugly was not the word that came to Rory's mind as she grabbed the damp towel and walked to his side. "Come here."

He leaned forward, and she lifted a hand to brush his dark hair back from his forehead. His gaze caught hers, and she paused, almost forgetting why she'd embarked on this task.

She dabbed at the paint just as she had with Hannah. The actions might have been the same, but Rory's response was completely different. Her hand trembled as she traced a path across Jamison's forehead, his temple and along one cheekbone. She lowered the towel but didn't back away, staying whisper close, as his gaze searched hers.

"Better?" he murmured.

"Not quite so ugly anymore." She'd meant the words as a tease, but the huskiness in her voice gave her away.

Hannah had grabbed the empty water bottle, seeming to enjoy making the thin plastic crackle and pop in her small hands. Crouched along the edge of the pathway, her interest soon turned to scooping loose dirt into the narrow container.

Rory had learned the little girl's attention didn't stay captured for long, but for now...

She brushed her lips against Jamison's, their equal height giving the illusion of equal footing until Jamison caught her face in his hands, took control and shattered any pretense of staying grounded.

It was a quick kiss. A prelude for what was to come. A promise of more...but enough to send her head spinning into the clouds, leaving her breathless and dizzy with desire. She didn't know if her feet would have actually left the earth, but Jamison held her fast. He caught her hips and pulled her into the cradle of his thighs.

The gazebo had always been her favorite place, and that was before. Now every time she closed her eyes, Rory would see Jamison leaning against the carved post, paint streaked across his forehead and a gleam in his eyes. His low voice would echo through the whisper of wind in the trees and Hannah's lilting laughter would ring out with the trilling call of the birds. Pizza would never taste the same again, and paint fumes would always bring her back to this moment and this man.

Her favorite place and her favorite people in the whole, whole world...

"Ryder's bachelor party is tomorrow night."

"I know, so is Lindsay's bachelorette party."

"Do I even want to know what goes on at a bachelorette party?"

"Probably not." Rory was touched Lindsay had invited her and had been looking forward to hanging out with a group of women who weren't pointing and whispering behind her back.

Ever since the night of the rodeo, she'd lost count of the conversations that had stopped the moment she stepped into a room or neared a group of Hillcrest employees. As usual Trisha Katzman was right in the middle, surrounded by her flock. Whenever the redhead spoke, the other women leaned in like hungry birds, eyes wide and mouths open, pecking over a tasty morsel of gossip as they whispered back and forth.

Thrusting the thought aside, she asked, "What do you have planned for Ryder's last night as a free man?"

"You know me, something wild and crazy."

Rory couldn't help but laugh at his deadpan delivery. "It's always the quiet ones you have to watch out for."

Jamison smirked a little. "Per the groom's specific instructions, we're having a guys' night out at the Clearville Bar and Grille for a debauched evening of pool, darts and beer."

"Hmm, if not for the beer, you could invite Ryder's son and a few of his school friends along."

"Oh, you are funny."

She was glad he thought so. The bachelor and bachelorette parties were among the last events leading up to the wedding. The rehearsal dinner was scheduled at Hillcrest House the evening before the wedding, and after that— After that, it would all be over.

Lindsay and Ryder's life as a married couple would just be starting, but her relationship with Jamison would come to an end.

A smarter woman might have tried to keep her distance, to guard her heart, but Rory didn't have that kind of strength. She did know she was right about one thing, though. Ending their relationship now wouldn't make her miss him any less, so she was determined to enjoy what time they had together now.

She was afraid she'd have plenty of time to be miserable later.

Jamison cleared his throat and glanced over to where Hannah was now sprinkling the collected dirt along the walkway. "I, um, talked to Ryder. His parents are watching Robbie and his cousins tomorrow night. He said they'd be happy to add a girl to the mix."

"Do you think Hannah will be okay staying with them?"

Jamison huffed out a sigh. "Ever since the night of the unicorn, Hannah's been asking when she can play with Robbie and his cousins again."

Rory laughed. "But that's a good thing, isn't it?"

"A good thing for Hannah...and I'm hoping a very good thing for us."

Their time alone since the night of the rodeo had been limited to stolen kisses when Hannah was preoccupied with some game of make-believe or in the evening after the little girl had gone to bed. But Jamison was careful not to go too far, pushing them both to the brink before pulling back from the edge.

If Rory didn't know better, she might have thought he was trying to drive her out of her mind.

But if Hannah was happy staying with a sitter for a night...

"Don't tell me," Rory said, keeping a light note in her voice despite the bass drum beating inside her chest, "you have something wild and crazy planned?"

"Oh, sweetheart, you have no idea."

Chapter Twelve

"Am I the only one who thinks this is a bad idea?" Rory's words fell on deaf ears as she and the rest of Lindsay's bridal party scrambled out of the SUV amid constant chattering and bursts of laughter.

"I'm afraid so," Sophia Pirelli Cameron said. The petite brunette met Rory's exasperated glance with a sympathetic look. "You've been out-Pirellied."

"I had no idea that was even a thing."

Sophia laughed. "When you have as much family in town as I do, you learn to go with the flow."

At the moment, the five women, including Sophia's sister-in-law, Debbie, were flowing toward the Clearville Bar and Grille, a local watering hole offering beer, chips, an assortment of burgers and every sport imaginable on large-screen TVs. The place was popular with locals and tourists alike, and for tonight, it was the hot spot for bachelor parties. As in Ryder's bachelor party.

The girls were supposed to be out for their own night on the town, but halfway to Redfield, Debbie had had the great idea of crashing the guys' night out. The exuberant blonde's enthusiasm was contagious, and it hadn't taken much convincing for Lindsay's future sister-in-law, Nina, to turn the car around and head back to Clearville, where all of their guys waited.

Well, not her guy.

Jamison would be there, of course, but the other women were all married or about to be married to the men inside. While she and Jamison...

"That's a pretty heavy sigh for a Saturday night," Sophia commented as the two of them fell into step a few paces behind Lindsay, Debbie and Nina, who were already racing toward the bar. "I don't suppose it has anything to do with a certain best man, does it?"

"Jamison is part of the wedding party and a guest at our hotel—"

"Not to mention single...and hot...at least according to Debbie and my cousin Theresa."

Rory groaned. "You're right. Your family really has taken over the town, haven't they?"

"Pretty much," Sophia said. "But what can I say? Clearville's home, and I'm glad to be back. I'm only sorry I stayed away so long."

Music and light spilled out from the open double doors leading into the bar. Their steps slowed as they neared the entrance. "Considering how much family you have here, why did you stay away?"

The brunette lifted a shoulder in an easy shrug. "Small towns have long memories. When I was in high school, I screwed up. I trusted the wrong person and did something I shouldn't, and when we got caught, I took the blame. I'm not proud of what happened, but the thing I regret the most is the guilt that drove a wedge between me and my family. I never should have let that happen, especially not when they forgave me long before I got around to forgiving myself."

I trusted the wrong person.

Boy, did Rory know how that felt! And maybe she had carried her guilt around for too long—when that was the only thing she'd done wrong.

"Thank you, Sophia."

The brunette shot her a curious glance. "For what?"

"For helping put the past into perspective."

"You're welcome, and while I'm doling out pearls of wisdom, let me tell you that trips to the past are best served with fruity cocktails."

Rory's laughter faded away as they stepped inside the bar and she spotted the combined bachelor and bachelorette parties gathered near the pool tables. Music blared from the jukebox in the corner, making it impossible to hear what they were saying. But even in the dim lighting and neon glow cast from the beer signs hanging on the walls, what she saw made her heart sink.

Ryder was furious. Lindsay stood in front of her fiancé, her pretty face distraught, as the rest of the bridal party milled awkwardly around the couple.

He couldn't be so upset because Lindsay had crashed his stag party! In all the time Rory had worked with the groom-to-be, he'd been nothing but laid-back and relaxed, happy with whatever made Lindsay happy. Watching them together, Rory had thought they were the perfect couple...

In an instant, she switched from member of the bachelorette party to wedding coordinator. There had to be something she could do to fix this!

Cutting through the crowd gathered in front of the bar, Rory reached Bryce Kincaid's side. "Bryce, what is going on?"

"One minute everything was fine, and then in the next—" Ryder's brother shook his head. "All I know is that I heard Ryder tell Jamison he's not sure if he even wants Jamison to be at the wedding, forget having him *in* the wedding."

Jamison? This was about *Jamison*?

A tearful Lindsay caught sight of Rory and hurried to her side. "This is awful! Jamison is the best man. Ryder's best friend! I know how much he wants Jamison standing beside him." She brushed the backs of her fingers beneath her eyes. "I'm not going to be so dramatic as to say Jamison's absence will ruin the wedding, but I know how much it will hurt Ryder if he's not there. Something like this could ruin their friendship."

"Do you know what the fight was about?"

"Other than me?" Lindsay asked with a sad little laugh. "No clue."

"Okay. You keep working on Ryder and see if he'll open up. I'll find Jamison. Between the two of us, they don't stand a chance."

"Thank you, Rory."

"Wedding coordinator to the rescue," she promised, glad to hear a genuine laugh from her friend as she gave her a quick hug.

Oh, Jamison, what did you do?

Turning to Bryce, she asked, "Do you know where Jamison is now?"

"He drove separately from the rest of us in case he had to leave early to pick up Hannah." At her questioning glance, he added, "I've already called my folks. They haven't heard from him, and Hannah's asleep on the couch after somehow talking my boys into watching a princess movie with her."

"I rode over with the rest of the bachelorette party—"

"I can give you a ride if you know where he might have gone."

"Let's start at the hotel."

Once Rory spotted Jamison's SUV in the parking lot, she convinced Bryce she could handle things from there. Faint moonlight lit the way to the lobby, but a gut feeling had her veering away from the elegant building and following a familiar path instead.

She ducked under the yellow caution tape barring the way to the gazebo. The elegant structure was draped in shadows, still and silent, and a dark figure sat hunched on the top step. Her heart ached at the loneliness, the isolation he seemed to have wrapped around him like a moth-eaten-yet-familiar blanket.

Oh, Jamison, she thought again. *What did you do?*

She set foot on the first step, noticing the six-pack of beer, and sank down beside him. Smoothing her skirt over her knees, she kept her gaze focused straight ahead as she asked, "Come here often?"

Jamison tipped his head back to take a swallow from the beer in his hand before stating, "I'm not even going to ask how you found me here."

"I think the better question would be *why* are you here?"

"I'm getting drunk," he said, the clarity of his words and the barely touched bottle belying his words. "Isn't that what tonight is all about?"

"Actually, tonight is about spending time with your best friend and celebrating his upcoming marriage."

"I don't think Ryder would call me his best friend anymore. Even though all I was trying to do was to look out for him."

A bad feeling sinking into the pit of her stomach, Rory asked, "Look out for him how?"

"I told him it wasn't too late—"

"To call off the wedding?" She reared back in shock and might have tumbled from the step if he hadn't steadied her with his free hand.

"No, no, not to call it off. Just to have one of the lawyers at the firm draft a prenup."

"Oh, Jamison."

"I didn't think he'd—I'm trying to protect him, you know? Isn't that what a best man—a best *friend*—does?"

"I think a best man should be happy his friend has found the love of his life."

Wincing, he ran a hand through his hair. "I tried to have a good time. I did, but all I could think about was that I'd been there, done that, and look how it ended."

"Been there?"

"I was best man at Ryder's last wedding, too."

"Oh."

"Yeah. And that time, I did keep my mouth shut, even though I sensed Ryder was feeling pressured into the marriage. I told myself it was cold feet and everything would work out."

"And everything did work out."

He shot her an incredulous look. "They were miserable together. They ended up getting divorced."

"Yes, so Ryder and Lindsay can get married now."

"You are incredible."

"Thank you."

"Not a compliment. You can't be that naive."

Rory sucked in a lungful of cool night air and tried not to let that arrow strike her heart. He thought she was naive for believing Ryder and Lindsay's love was meant to last. How foolish would he think she was for falling for him when she'd known all along their relationship was destined to end?

Keeping her voice steady despite the trembling inside, she said, "Believing in love isn't being naive any more than being cynical makes you smart. All it does is blind you to the good things in life. I don't know anything about Ryder's first marriage, but I do know he's crazy about Lindsay."

"Lindsay kept his son from him for nine *years*! Ryder didn't even know Robbie existed. At least Monica only—" Cutting himself off, Jamison shook his head and took another drink.

"What did Monica do?" Rory asked, her words blending in with the rustle of wind through the trees, the distant rush of waves against the shore.

For a long moment, she didn't think he would answer, that he would keep his words—like his heart—locked up in the past. But finally, he started to speak. "We'd been fighting a lot, so much that I was afraid it would start to affect Hannah."

"And you didn't want that…not after the way you'd grown up."

"It's the last thing I wanted for Hannah. I did my best to ignore the worst of Monica's habits—the extreme shopping, the time she'd spend out with friends instead of at home with Hannah, her complaints that I was the one who spent too much time at work to be a good husband and father. Although she was right about that…"

Jamison still didn't know if his marriage had failed because of all the time he put in at work or if he put in all that time at work because his marriage was failing. But he did know Hannah had paid the price.

"Jamison—"

Ignoring her softly voiced protest, he continued, "Before long, Monica and I couldn't seem to be in the same room together without arguing, and I felt like I had no choice. I moved out. We called it a separation, but I think we both knew we wouldn't be getting back together. I don't know why I didn't ask for a divorce right then."

"Maybe because you still were holding out hope you would work things out."

Jamison gave a rough laugh, his hand tightening on the beer bottle. "Well, if that is the reason, it was a foolish hope. We might not have fought as often, but when we did, it was as bad, if not worse. That's when she started keeping me from seeing Hannah. It was small things at first. Dropping her off a few minutes late, picking her up early. But before long, she was canceling visits altogether. Hannah was sleeping or not feeling well or had a playdate with friends. One excuse after another until I was lucky to see Hannah once a month instead of every weekend."

It was his father who had warned him not to make the same mistakes he had. "I let your mother convince me you were better off without me," he'd told Jamison. "I was never going to be rich or successful. I was never going to be the kind of man she would be proud of. But the one regret I have is that I didn't fight as hard as I could for you, Jamie. You are rich and successful, but I can promise you, none of that will mean a thing if you don't have that little girl in your life."

Rory shifted closer to him, slipping the cold, hard bottle from his hand and replacing it with the warm, soft reassurance of her own. "And that was wrong of Monica, but—"

"That's not all she did, Rory." Jamison had to take a deep breath to get out the words, buried deep in his memory where he tried his damnedest not to think about them. "I couldn't let things continue the way they were going. So I told Monica I was filing for divorce. I was prepared for her to go ballistic, but she barely reacted. I left that day feeling this huge sense of relief and went on an out-of-town business trip, thinking everything would work out. I should have known better."

The wind picked up, drawing a curtain of clouds over the full moon. Dark memories crouched in the shadows, trying to drag him back into the past, but Jamison held on tight to Rory's hand, her touch, her presence keeping him present.

He thought of the first time he saw her, how her smile, her beauty had warmed him like a summer day... She was his sunshine, his ray of light.

"I tried calling while I was gone, and when she didn't call me back, I started to get this bad feeling. She'd been so calm when I left, acting so out of character... I tried her parents to see if they could get ahold of her, but they couldn't reach her, either. Finally, I left in the middle of a meeting and took the first flight I could get home. I didn't know what I would find."

"Oh, Jamison."

Even though he had moved out, he'd convinced Monica to allow him to keep a key in case of emergencies. "When I got there, everything was the same as when I left, and I felt foolish for overreacting. It's not like it was the first time Monica had avoided my calls. But then I found her phone on the counter. She never went anywhere without that phone."

He'd torn through the house after that, the missing items as telling as the phone she'd left behind. Suitcases, clothes, Hannah's favorite toys... "Monica was gone, and she'd taken Hannah with her."

"Jamison... I am so sorry. How awful for you to have to go through that!"

There was more. There was what happened the day of the accident, but Jamison couldn't bring himself to tell Rory about that. Couldn't watch the sympathy and understanding in her beautiful face fade into the condemnation he saw whenever he looked in the mirror.

"How long were they gone?"

"Almost four months. One hundred and seventeen days."

Gazing at his granite profile, Rory could still see the toll that time had taken on Jamison written in his tense jaw, the brackets around his mouth and the hand fisted at his side. Her heart ached for all he—and Hannah—had been through, emotion building inside her as she wished for something to say to wipe those bad memories away. Instead, she scooted closer to him on the step and rested her head on his shoulder.

"I know it doesn't sound like a long time—" he started.

"It sounds like an eternity," she protested and felt a small sense of victory when Jamison sighed and some of that tension eased out of him. And when he leaned his head against hers, Rory wished this was a moment she could make last.

"Between the separation and the time she was gone, I only saw Hannah a handful of times in almost eight months. She'd grown so much, when I first saw her in— when I first saw her again, I hardly recognized her."

"But all of that happened to you and Monica. It didn't happen to—"

Us.

Monica had let him down, betraying him in the worst way possible, but Rory wanted him to know he could count on her. That he could trust her with his heart, and even more important, he could trust her with his daughter. She would never let either of them down.

"To Lindsay and Ryder."

"I don't know how he can forgive her."

But it wasn't Lindsay Jamison needed to forgive. He needed to find a way to forgive himself.

"It's not your fault."

But instead of soothing his pain, her words caused Jamison to jerk away. He vaulted off the steps only to turn back and point an accusing finger at her—as if condemning her for trusting him, for loving him. "You don't know, Rory—"

"I know you." She stood slowly before she deliberately made her way down the steps. "I might not know the man you were, but I know the man you are. A good father, a good friend, a man who—"

"A man who killed his wife!"

"What?" Rory stumbled on the final step, but this time Jamison wasn't there to catch her. She regained her balance at the last second, her legs, her entire body trembling at the force of his words. Words that couldn't be true. "I don't understand. Monica died in a car accident. Were you—were you the one driving?"

His arm fell to his side, and his chin dropped to his chest. "I was a thousand miles away."

"Then how—"

"Monica called me. When she figured out I had a detective looking for her, she called me. We were yelling at each other, ugly, hateful things—and then I heard her scream."

"Oh, my God. You heard the accident?"

"Heard it? I *caused* it."

"Oh, Jamison, you can't believe that! You know it isn't true. Monica called *you*. You didn't know she was behind the wheel."

"I should have. I should have realized she'd take Hannah and run again—"

"Maybe, maybe you could have guessed she'd do that. But you couldn't know that she would crash."

He closed his eyes as if that could block a truth guilt wouldn't allow him to believe. He might not listen and he didn't want to see, but Rory could still make him *feel*. She lifted her hands to his face, and the scrape of his late-night stubble sent chills up her arms. The sensation was as powerful as if he'd run his jaw over her sensitive skin from her wrist all the way to her shoulder.

And she knew in the split second before she raised her mouth to his, that this kiss wouldn't be the caring, consoling kiss she intended. But then their lips met, and she stopped worrying about what the kiss was supposed to be and focused on what it *was*.

Raw. Intense. So close to perfection, she could have been dreaming. But the tension in Jamison's body, the lingering anguish, was all too real. The need to take that pain away had Rory parting her lips beneath his, as if she could somehow draw out the darkness trapped inside him.

Touching and tasting, the kiss grew more and more heated, and the air seemed to sizzle around them. It burned in her lungs until she had to break the kiss and gasp for breath.

"Rory." He groaned her name in what might have been a protest, but the plea in his rough voice and a tiny thread of hope let her know how much he wanted to believe.

"There are a million things you could have done differently then, but there's not a single one you can do now to change what happened."

"So I'm just supposed to forget?"

"No, you're supposed to remember. To remember how lucky you are that Hannah survived and that she's okay."

"I am. You have no idea how damn grateful I am that she wasn't badly hurt."

"I know. I know." Rory swallowed hard, knowing the words she needed to speak and knowing how hard they would be for Jamison to hear. "And you have Monica to thank...because no matter how angry she was, how determined to run, she still took the time to buckle Hannah into her car seat. To make sure your daughter was as safe as possible in case of an accident no one could see coming."

His fingers flexed at her hips, and Rory tensed, waiting for him to push her away. To reject her and the forgiveness she wanted for him. Instead, he pulled her body to his. Close, then closer until she could hear his ragged breathing and feel his heart thundering. Until she resented every article of clothing, every millimeter of distance separating them.

"I can't. I know you want me to forgive Monica, but I can't."

"It isn't about what I want, Jamison. It's about what you need."

"I need you, Rory. All I need is you."

He swept her up in his arms, but instead of carrying her away from the gazebo, he climbed the stairs to the shadowed platform. It was dark, and the secluded gazebo seemed a million miles away from the hotel and its slumbering guests. As he sank down onto the top step—the one with their hidden initials carved in the wood—and drew her into his lap, no one else existed outside the world they created for each other.

He murmured her name against her mouth, her cheek, her throat. Each husky whisper sent shivers running up and down her spine. The seductive, potent promises set off tiny explosions along her nerve endings—fizzy and sparkling and all building to a grand finale. She tugged his shirt from his jeans and shoved her hands beneath the soft material. The tight muscles and smooth skin of his back made her greedy for more.

His eyes blazed at the proof of her impatience, and he

reached behind his back with one hand to pull the shirt over his head. She smothered her startled laughter at the unexpected move against his neck, breathing in the scent of his skin and the anticipation of what was to come.

With his shirt gone, she had the freedom to explore his broad shoulders, muscled chest and stomach, first with her eyes and then with her hands. His hair-roughened skin tickled her palms, but it was Jamison who flinched as she worked the button on his jeans.

"Rory." He caught her hand, his grip a little rough as he held her fingers against his rock-hard abdomen. He didn't ask the question, but the words were written in his glittering gaze.

I'm leaving...

Leaning forward, she gave her answer as her lips found his. *You're still here...*

Their affair might not last, but Jamison seemed determined to make it one she would never forget as his hands slid beneath her skirt and he set out to brand every inch of her body. He stripped away her panties and found her wet and waiting for him. Heat flooded her bloodstream, a tidal wave of desire that washed away the worries of what tomorrow might bring and left her bathed in his kiss, his touch...

Until the tide turned, and Rory was the one painting kisses over his chest, shoulders and stomach. She'd studied dozens of swatches over the years—paints, fabrics, ribbons—but she'd never before realized that kisses came in colors. The innocence of pink, the glorious revelry of gold, the rich decadence of red...

She'd nearly completed a rainbow when Jamison stopped her. She muttered a protest that was silenced when he reached for protection and then lifted her above him. Her body sank onto his, and Rory welcomed him just as she'd welcomed his kiss, his touch, his heartache. Her arms and legs wrapped tight, never wanting to let him go...

With his hands at her hips, he slowly began to move, increasing a pace destined to drive her wild. Her body rose and fell with every thrust, and a kaleidoscope of colors burst behind her eyelids as the pleasure broke, showering down over them in a burst of fireworks.

His breathing was still rough in her ear, his heart pounding against hers, when Rory pressed her lips to his shoulder, fighting a smile he evidently felt against his skin. "What's so funny?"

"I was thinking we should do something to celebrate the gazebo's reopening, but this is so much better than anything I had in mind!"

Chapter Thirteen

Jamison woke slowly, blinking against the early-morning light. The sun streamed through the curtains, and he suffered a moment's disorientation. He never slept this late. Hannah never let him sleep this late. At the thought of his daughter, his eyes flew open and took in the unfamiliar, feminine surroundings. Lace curtains. White wicker furniture. Pale pink walls and sheets embellished with tiny pink roses. At the sound of a soft sigh, the memories from the night before came rushing back.

Rory. In his arms at the gazebo last night. Rory. In bed with him this morning.

Wide-awake now, he rolled his head on the pillow. They'd made their way back to her cottage after leaving the gazebo, stumbling through the darkened rooms before falling into her bed and making love a second time. She slept on her side facing him, one hand cradled against her cheek. Her dark hair spilled in disarray across the pillowcase, her eyelashes forming soft shadows against her cheeks. Sheer amazement filled him. He'd never seen a lovelier or more amazing sight.

He felt the ridiculous urge to wake her, as if that might somehow prove last night hadn't been a dream.

As if she could read his thoughts, her eyelids fluttered, then drifted open. Unlike his momentary confusion, her eyes were clear. "Morning," she whispered.

"Hi," he murmured, almost afraid to break the silence.

"What time is it?"

"Early," he insisted, ignoring his previous admission.

She smiled at his white lie. "Not that early. When are you supposed to pick up Hannah?"

"We didn't have a set time, since no one knew how late we'd stay out."

Reaching out, she cupped his face in her hand. "You know you have to make things right with Ryder."

Jamison didn't want to lose his oldest and best friend, but Ryder wasn't first on his mind as he pressed a kiss into Rory's palm. "I didn't plan for this, you know."

"Uh-oh." Her smile trembled a little as she tucked the sheet beneath her arms. "Do I hear another 'do the right thing' speech coming?"

"Too late for that," he sighed.

"But not too late for this." Leaning forward, her dark hair framing her face, she brushed her lips against his. The gentle, giving kiss still had the power to kick his pulse into overdrive and send desire crashing through his veins.

"Rory..."

"I know you're leaving, Jamison." Was it his imagination or was the shine in her blue eyes the glitter of tears? Before he could know for sure, she ducked her head again, punctuating her words with kisses on his face, his throat, his chest. "But not today...and not tomorrow..."

And before long, leaving Clearville—leaving Rory—was the last thing on his mind.

An hour later, Jamison pulled up in front of the Kincaid residence. Ryder's parents lived outside town in a ranch-style house with a wraparound porch and lush green front yard. The sounds of laughter and a dog barking filled the air as he headed for the front door.

"Kids are all out back." Ryder stepped through a side gate, coffee mug in hand, and let the door slam shut behind him. "Hannah has the boys playing some kind of game where she's a princess and they're trying to rescue her from a dragon. Who in this case is my brother's Border collie."

"Sounds like they're being pretty good sports about the whole thing."

Ryder shrugged as he climbed the steps to the porch. "Robbie's been begging for a dog, so any game that includes Cowboy is one he's up for."

Jamison opened his mouth, the apology stalling in his throat. "Seems like you survived last night."

"Yeah, it was a real blast." Ryder's poker face folded slightly as a wry smile kicked up one corner of his mouth. "Especially once the bridal party showed up."

"So that's what happened." He'd been too caught up in the moment last night to wonder how Rory had found out about the argument at the bachelor party.

"Huh?"

"It's—nothing. I was an ass last night."

Ryder took his time, lifting the mug, blowing on the steaming dark roast, taking a swallow before saying, "Got that right."

Jamison sighed. He was going to make him say the words. "I'm sorry. I know you love Lindsay and she loves you, and I…hope everything works out."

His friend tipped his mug in Jamison's direction. "But you don't think it will."

"Dammit, Ryder, I'm trying really hard not to get into another fight with you."

"Good thing, since I'd kick your ass."

"And I'd sue yours until you didn't have a penny to your name."

Ryder smirked, and Jamison figured they could call their insult battle a draw. His friend lifted the mug for another drink, and Jamison noticed the gold trophy and the words *World's Greatest Father* on the side.

"You want to know how I can forgive Lindsay? The truth is, that's the only way I could expect her to forgive me. The only way I could forgive myself."

It's not your fault. Rory's words whispered through his mind. *And you have Monica to thank...*

He couldn't. Maybe if he had Rory's capacity for love, for hope, for forgiveness, he could forgive Monica. But he was a man who lived the law—right and wrong, black or white.

Jamison shook his head. "You didn't do anything wrong! You didn't know Lindsay was pregnant."

"I didn't want to know," Ryder stressed. "I slept with her. I knew the baby could be mine—forget what the Clearville grapevine had to say. But I had plans, big plans, and you better believe being a teenage dad wasn't part of them." He rubbed his thumb over the trophy emblem on the mug. "That's not an easy thing to admit, even now, but it was something I had to face when Lindsay told me about Robbie. Something we both had to get over in order to move on."

And he was moving on. To a life with the woman he loved with a confidence and faith Jamison...envied. "I really was trying to look out for you."

"I get it. I do. Your head was in the right place."

"Isn't the expression your *heart* was in the right place?"

"Oh, hell, no. Your heart's all messed up, dude."

"What is that supposed to mean?"

"Just that half the stuff you were saying was way more about what's going on with you than anything to do with me."

Bits and pieces of his argument echoed across the lush green lawn.

You have to protect yourself.

You made a mistake before.

Don't leave yourself open to getting hurt again.

Jamison swore under his breath. "When did you end up being the smart one in this friendship?"

"I was always the smart one. Playing the dumb jock was how I got all the girls."

"You are so full of it."

Jogging down the porch steps, Ryder spoke over his shoulder. "Yep. But I'm right."

He'd always had a bit of showman in him back in his college football days, and Jamison couldn't help thinking his friend hadn't lost his touch as he followed him around to the side of the house. Ryder pushed the gate open wide, and Jamison saw what was behind door number one.

In the middle of a green tree-lined lawn, Hannah held a beat-up red Frisbee over her head, running and laughing as the black-and-white dog and three boys chased after her.

Her pure joy grabbed hold of Jamison, and he didn't want to let go. Didn't want to step back from the emotion pouring through him. He wanted to embrace it for all it was worth, and he only wished he had Rory at his side to share in this miracle.

Hillcrest's magic touches whoever needs it most.

She was magic. She was his princess and fairy godmother

rolled into one, and Jamison didn't know what he would do without her in his life.

As if reading his thoughts, Ryder said, "You have a good thing going with Rory, Jamison." At Jamison's questioning glance, his friend added, "Your daughter isn't exactly a vault when it comes to Miss Rory and how much time you are all spending together."

"Rory's...amazing. She's been so good for Hannah."

"She's been good for *you*. That's what's made the biggest change with Hannah. Kids are smarter than most adults give them credit for. She's taking her cues from you. If you're happy..."

"She's happy," Jamison finished, but he still wasn't sure he believed it. Or maybe he was too afraid to believe it. Too afraid he couldn't be this happy in San Francisco. That he wouldn't be this happy anywhere that Rory wasn't. "When we get back home..."

"What happens when you get back?"

"I don't know." Hannah had come so far, and maybe Ryder was right. Maybe he too had taken some serious strides when it came to being the kind of dad Hannah deserved, but without Rory...he didn't know if he could keep going in the right direction.

And yet... "Rory and I both agreed. After the wedding, we go our separate ways. No hard feelings." And no broken hearts.

It didn't take a genius to figure out a woman like Rory wanted more than a short-term fling. The woman lived and breathed weddings and had made her belief in romance and a love of a lifetime clear.

All of which asked the question of what the hell she was doing with him.

He was jaded, cynical, so wary of love he'd almost blown a longtime friendship because he wasn't ready to believe Ryder had found a love that would last beyond the honeymoon stage.

"So that's it?" Ryder twirled the now-empty mug around by the handle, and Jamison had the feeling his friend was thinking of chucking it at his head. "You meet this amazing woman and you're going to kiss her good-bye?"

Thoughts of kisses and goodbyes took him right back to Rory's bed that morning. Their relationship was temporary. It had to be. They'd agreed. And nothing this good could last.

He might not know much about fairy tales, but he knew what happened when the clock struck midnight. Their magical night would be over.

"What else am I supposed to do, Ryder? My life is back in San Francisco."

"Your *job* is back in San Francisco. Don't fool yourself by calling that a life. And if you're going to walk away from the best thing that ever happened to you, at least be honest about the reasons why."

"I wanna see Miss Rory!"

Jamison sucked in a breath, struggling for patience—with his daughter and with himself. *He* wanted to see Rory. He wanted to talk to her about his conversation with Ryder, to let her know he was back on track as Ryder's best man and as his best friend. He wanted to thank her for that... and for a whole lot more.

A handful of hours had passed since he'd left her bed that morning, and his eagerness to see her again surprised him. Worried him.

I won't miss you any less if you leave tomorrow.

He wasn't leaving tomorrow. The wedding was Saturday and his reservation lasted through the weekend, but he couldn't deny their time together was coming to an end.

He wasn't worried so much about missing Rory as he was about finding the strength to leave.

"Daddy!"

"Hannah—" Catching himself before he could snap at his daughter, he reminded her, "We can't see Rory right now. She's working."

She'd told him about the small afternoon wedding taking place in the rose garden. She'd spent most of the day yesterday preparing for the event in the hours leading up to the bachelorette party.

"But I wanna tell her about the sleepover! We played games and watched princess movies and Mrs. Kincaid doesn't know how to make smiley-face oatmeal, but she made smiley-face pancakes instead!"

Pancakes... Jamison closed his eyes with a sigh. That explained the sugar rush that had the little girl bouncing around their suite like the Energizer Bunny. "Why don't we go outside for a walk?"

"To the gazebo?" Hannah asked, her brown eyes wide.

What kind of father was he that he wanted to keep the memory of his night with Rory and the gazebo to himself? That he wasn't ready to see the magical spot in the full light of day?

"How about down to the beach instead?"

"Can we hop like bunnies?"

"If we do will it make you super sleepy so you take a big nap this afternoon?"

Hannah wrinkled her forehead. "I don't think bunnies take naps, Daddy."

"Of course they don't," he muttered as they headed out of the suite and into the hallway. All the time wondering at the odds of convincing his hopping daughter to be a giant sloth instead.

With Hannah tugging at his hand, Jamison stepped out of the lobby and into the sunny, cloudless day. A slight breeze blew off the ocean, cooling the sun's rays and adding a hint of sea salt to the air. He couldn't help giving a slight chuckle at the first thought that came to mind.

It really was the perfect day for a wedding.

As they headed down the path leading to the rocky shoreline, a familiar sound rang out in an unfamiliar setting. Reaching into his pocket, he pulled out his cell phone. He still kept the thing charged, carried it with him everywhere, even though away from the hotel, he rarely had reception.

In San Francisco he could count on one hand the number of times he didn't respond to a call within half an hour. Here, he'd gotten used to missed calls, lengthy messages and unreturned emails. Most of the time, he waited until the evening when Hannah was asleep to respond.

But not last night.

Last night, San Francisco and the law firm had been the last things on his mind.

But when he saw the name on the screen, he swiped his thumb to answer the call.

"Jeez, Porter, where the hell are you, the dark side of the moon?" his friend and fellow lawyer Donnie Lipinski demanded. "I've been trying to get ahold of you for days!"

"Sorry, cell coverage is pretty spotty around here."

His friend swore so loudly Jamison automatically looked to Hannah who was tugging on his arm. "Give me a second, will you, Hannah Banana?"

"I wanna see Rory!"

"In a minute."

Hannah dropped to her butt in a pout, arms crossed

over her chest and bottom lip stuck out as far as it would go. "Count to one hundred and I'll be ready to go," he promised.

Lifting the phone back to his ear, Jamison caught Donnie midstream. "...middle-of-nowhere vacation?"

"One! Two! Three!"

Hannah's counting reached an almost-obnoxious volume, and Jamison covered his ear with his free hand. "I'm here for a friend's wedding," he reminded Donnie.

"A wedding lasts what, a day? Maybe two if you get suckered into going to the rehearsal dinner. You've been there almost two weeks." Lowering his voice, he added, "Do you know how many clients Martinez and Harris have met with in two weeks? And word has it Martinez grabbed the Langstone account."

Jamison took his turn swearing, though he was careful to do it under his breath. The firm encouraged competition between its employees, with a "may the best man win" mentality. Langstone Communications was a coveted account, one he'd thought he had a good shot of landing... two weeks ago.

"They're pushing hard toward the finish line, and you're still stuck in the blocks, man."

Hannah finally reached twenty, and Jamison dropped his free hand. "I needed to come here, Don. It was important."

"More important than your career?" Incredulity filled his friend's voice, as if he couldn't image what could top that. The thrill of the chase, the euphoria of landing the biggest, brightest account had been a rush beyond anything Jamison could imagine.

But he never could have imagined a woman like Rory. Making love to her, kissing her, hell, even making her smile made him happier than any client, any account ever had.

But he'd been a lawyer for years, and everything he felt for Rory was so new, so fragile. And hadn't the personal relationships in his life taught him that nothing lasted? His feelings for Rory would fade, and he would need the comfort, the security of his career to fall back on. "I'll be back on Monday," he told Donnie.

His friend snorted. "Who knows how many accounts your competition will have brought in by then? Forget the promotion—you'll be lucky to still have a job."

Jamison opened his mouth to retort, but Donnie had hung up. As much as he loved modern technology, what he wouldn't give for an old-fashioned phone he could slam back into its cradle right now. Instead, he dropped the cell into his pocket.

He wasn't in danger of losing his job. Donnie was busting his balls with that comment. But the promotion... Yeah, he had a feeling he could kiss that goodbye.

You're destined for bigger things, Jamison. Never forget that. Never settle for less when you can take more.

His mother's words echoed through his thoughts as he ran a hand through his hair. He didn't want to end up like her—grasping and grappling to hold on to something fleeting that had already passed him by. He'd worked hard for that partnership, dammit! He'd put in the long hours, the nights, the weekends. He'd given his all! He'd sacrificed—

He'd sacrificed his marriage just to be considered.

What would he be expected to sacrifice to win it all?

Reaching into his pocket, he powered down his phone.

"Hey, Hannah—" His shoes crunched on the loose gravel as he turned. "Are you ready—"

His words—his heart—stopped at the sight of the empty path behind him.

Chapter Fourteen

"Hannah!" He called her name, but this was no game of hide-and-seek with his daughter giggling, hardly out of sight, a few feet away. She was gone. "Hannah!"

He froze, unsure where to go, what to do...but then he knew.

Hannah had gone to find Rory.

He had to believe that, just like he had to believe he'd find the two of them together. He couldn't bear to think anything else. The rose garden wasn't far from the front entrance of the hotel, and he ran the distance in record time. His heart pounded in his ears so loudly he could barely hear the strains of a harp floating on the air. But that sound and the activity around the wedding had to have drawn Hannah to the one spot where Rory was sure to be.

She *had* to be there.

He stopped short as he rounded a curve, his shoes skidding beneath him. Two dozen people filled the white chairs lining the lawn, all focused on the couple standing beneath the delicate arched trellis. He scanned the crowd but didn't see Rory. Didn't see Hannah.

The bride's tremulous voice barely carried to the back row. It was all Jamison could do to not hold his peace and to start calling out for his daughter...

"Psst, Daddy."

At first, he thought he'd imaged the faint whisper blending in with the breeze rustling through the trees. That the sound had come from one of the guests, murmuring under their breath about the bride or her dress or the ceremony. But then he heard it again.

"*Psst*, Daddy! Over here!"

The call was louder this time, enough for a few heads in the back row to turn his way. Jamison paid them no attention as he scanned the garden off to his right, where he finally spotted golden curls amid the verdant green bushes and red roses.

"Hannah."

Too relieved to have found her, Jamison didn't care about making a scene as he wound his way through the fragrant bushes until he could crouch down at his daughter's side and yank her into his arms. "Hannah, what are you doing? You know better than to go off without me!"

Her lower lip sticking out in a pout, she said, "I wanted to see Miss Rory's wedding."

"Hannah, this isn't Rory's wedding."

"Uh-huh," his daughter insisted. "See? She's right over there."

Jamison followed his daughter's outstretched hand and spotted Rory standing off to the side. His breath caught at the sight of her—her hands clasped in front of her chest and a beaming smile on her face. No one was supposed to be more beautiful than a bride on her wedding day, but as far as Jamison was concerned, no woman was more beautiful than Rory—ever.

Her outfit—a pale yellow sweater and narrow cream-colored skirt—was a little more sedate and businesslike than the flowery dresses she usually wore, and her hair was caught back in a professional-looking bun. But nothing she wore could ever downplay how stunning she was, and that was only on the outside.

Her inner beauty—her kindness, her compassion, her caring—that would shine through even in the darkest moments. Wasn't that why his first instinct when Hannah was missing was to run to Rory? Yes, he'd figured that Hannah had gone to find her, but even more than that, *he* had wanted to find Rory. To have her tell him that everything would be all right. To make it all better, the way she'd made everything in his life better.

And he couldn't help wondering if he was only fooling himself. If his feelings for Rory were destined to fade, then why did they grow stronger every time they were together?

"You know, we've never had a Hillcrest House wedding crashed before." Up until a minute ago, Rory wasn't sure how she'd feel the next time she saw Jamison. She hadn't imagined she'd be fighting laughter, but she found herself doing just that as she confronted the guilty-looking duo crouched at the back of the rose garden.

"Look, Daddy! It's Miss Rory!"

"So I see." His silver gaze swept over Rory with an intimacy and something…*more* that left her trembling in her sensible shoes. The wedding guests were focused on the bride and groom, but it still wouldn't do for her to launch herself into Jamison's arms in the middle of the ceremony. Even if she wanted to…

The soloist had started singing about the power of love,

providing enough ambient noise for Rory to feel comfortable murmuring, "You're not planning to rush the aisle when the pastor asks if anyone objects to this wedding, are you?"

"I wouldn't be anywhere near this ceremony if a certain someone—" he landed a pointed gaze on his oblivious daughter "—hadn't decided she wanted to come to your wedding."

"*My* wedding?"

"That's what she said."

"So this is my fault?"

"Clearly. My daughter is obsessed."

"With weddings?"

"I wish it were that simple."

As much as Rory wanted to deny she was a complication in Jamison's life, it was hard to do when his daughter scrambled over to take her hand. "Did you see the flower girl, Miss Rory?" Hannah asked. "She had a blue basket for her flowers and ribbons in her hair and she went like this!" Throwing out an arm, she exuberantly mimicked the other girl's flower-tossing technique.

Raising an eyebrow, Jamison murmured, "Was she throwing rose petals or a ninety-five-mile-an-hour fastball?"

"You hush," Rory scolded under her breath but with a smile. "I did see her, Hannah. But you don't have to lurk in the bushes."

"Are you sure?" Jamison asked. "As you pointed out, we aren't guests."

"You're my guests. Wedding coordinator's prerogative. Besides, it's not like the bride and groom will notice."

The young couple only had eyes for each other, and Rory led Jamison and Hannah closer in time for her favorite part.

"As long as we both shall live."

The tall, thin pastor beamed as he announced, "I now pronounce you husband and wife. You may kiss your bride."

The guests burst into applause as the groom cupped his bride's face and pressed his lips to hers in a kiss that was as much of a vow as the words he'd spoken.

It was a moment that would never get old, no matter how many weddings she witnessed, and one that never failed to bring tears to her eyes. The love, the hope, the promise of a future where two lives joined together as one... Her heart was filled with so much emotion, she couldn't stop some of it from overflowing.

She was struggling somewhat blindly with the clasp on the tiny clutch hanging from her wrist when Jamison's hand flashed in front of her face. Rory blinked, dislodging a tear or two, when she saw what he was holding out to her.

Snatching the tissue, she touched it to the corners of her eyes, trying not to do too much damage to her makeup. "Don't make fun. I always cry at weddings."

"Tears of joy that all the hard work is over?"

"No!" Her protest faded into laughter as she admitted, "Well, maybe. A little."

"I've also started carrying wet wipes if you really feel the need to break down."

"Hmm, those would have come in handy at the rodeo. Goes to show you're learning."

A muscle twitched in his jaw as he glanced down at his daughter. "She got away from me, Rory. I was on the phone. I swear I only turned away for a second, and when I looked back..."

She could only imagine the panic that must have raced like wildfire through Jamison's veins. Hannah's disappearance, even for a few minutes, must have taken him back to those long, agonizing months when his daughter had been gone and he'd had no idea when or if he'd see her again.

"Look at her now, Jamison." The little girl was focused on the ceremony taking place, throwing her arm out and tossing imaginary flower petals. "She's fine."

"No thanks to me."

"Jamison…"

"I don't know if I can do this, Rory. To be the kind of father Hannah deserves. I've already made so many mistakes. I wasn't there when she needed me most—"

"You're here now."

"But when I get back home…"

Jamison raked a hand through his hair. How was he supposed to juggle being a full-time father and full-time lawyer when he couldn't keep an eye on his daughter during a five-minute phone call?

"You can do this." Rory caught his hand in hers, her blue eyes shining with the faith that had been there from the start. A faith that made him believe he could do anything…as long as she was by his side.

"I can't—I can't do this without you. I don't want to do this without you," he blurted out. "I don't want to say goodbye."

"What?"

Pulling Rory into his arms, he pressed his forehead against hers. "After Ryder and Lindsay's wedding, I don't want that to be the end."

"Jamison, what—what are you saying?"

"Rory, I—we can make this work, right? Somehow?" He heard the desperation in his own voice but couldn't make the words stop spilling over one another. "We can call and text and maybe I can make it up here for Labor Day weekend…"

"Labor Day," she echoed weakly.

"We're good together, Rory. I want to give our relationship a chance."

Reaching up, she traced her fingers along his jaw, her touch tender, but her smile as sad as he'd ever seen. "Labor Day is a holiday, Jamison. Not a relationship."

"Rory—"

"We agreed, remember? When this is over, we say goodbye."

He stepped back, his hands dropping to his sides. She was turning him down? Sticking to the rules as if this was some kind of game they were playing?

"You can't mean that."

"I know you're scared, Jamison."

"Scared?"

"Of taking care of Hannah on your own."

Scared? Hell, he was terrified! But that wasn't why he wanted Rory in his life…was it? Okay, maybe his words had come across like a knee-jerk reaction to the panic rushing through him, but he'd still meant them.

"Miss Rory," Hannah piped in, breaking the moment. "Are you crying?"

Lifting her chin and turning her face away from him, she murmured, "Just a little." More now than when the couple had spoken their vows a few minutes earlier.

Vows joining two lives as one, to have and to hold, from this day forward… Vows of forever.

Not for a weekend. Not for a holiday.

Was he really surprised Rory had turned him down when he'd offered so much less than she deserved?

Gazing up at the two adults, the little girl said, "You hafta kiss her, Daddy. Like when my tummy didn't feel good. You kissed me and the next day—" Hannah threw her arms out wide "—I was all better."

"Listen to your daughter, Jamison." Rory offered him

another sad yet tender smile. "You can do this. You already know how to make it all better."

If this was better, Jamison thought as he followed his daughter's instructions and gave Rory a heartbreaking kiss that already felt too much like goodbye, he'd sure as hell hate to see what he could do to make things worse.

Hannah twirled back and forth in the middle of the bridal shop, the full skirt swishing around her knees. The cream-colored taffeta with its burgundy velvet sash and hint of matching lace at the hem fit perfectly. "Do I look like a real princess?"

"The prettiest princess ever." Rory and Hannah had met up with Lindsay at the shop to double-check the alterations and pick up the dress. The little girl beamed back, and her joy was enough to bring the sting of tears to Rory's eyes.

The days leading up to Ryder and Lindsay's wedding were the best and worst of Rory's life. She lived each day they were together—whether it was window-shopping in town, having a picnic at the gazebo, buying clothes for Hannah. But a part of her mourned the moment she closed her eyes, knowing each morning meant one day closer to Jamison and Hannah leaving.

But, oh, those nights...when Jamison pulled her into his arms, determined to remind her just how *good* they were together...

Making love with him was so magical, so amazing, Rory almost gave in. Almost agreed to what he offered. To late-night phone calls, video chats between meetings, the occasional stolen weekend. And she would have—if he'd told her he loved her.

"I think I'm the one who's supposed to tear up at this part," Lindsay said gently as she handed Rory a tissue once Hannah went to change back into her regular clothes.

"Although I can't blame you. If I didn't know better, I wouldn't even think that was the same girl from just a few weeks ago."

Rory dabbed at her eyes. "Time here in Clearville has done wonders for her."

"*You* have done wonders for her. For her and for Jamison."

She crumpled the tissue in her hand. Oh, how she wanted to believe Jamison had changed but, forcing a laugh, she said, "The same Jamison who wanted Ryder to get a prenup?"

Lindsay gave her a chiding look along with another tissue. "The same Jamison who apologized to Ryder and to me. He was looking out for Ryder—I can't really blame him for that."

He was a good friend, a good father, a good man... Was it any wonder she'd fallen so in love with him?

"We agreed. When our time together is over, we say goodbye."

"Well, it's not like it was written in stone. You can change your mind. Something tells me you *have* changed your mind."

"It doesn't matter if I've changed my mind. Not if Jamison hasn't changed his."

"And you're so sure he hasn't?"

I can't do this without you.

She'd heard it before from grateful brides and grooms. How Rory was the glue bringing together all the thousands of tiny details that made up a wedding. How they never could have managed it all on their own. But then the big day was over, and the newly married couples went on with their lives.

It would be the same for Jamison and Hannah. They would go back to San Francisco, back to their lives.

Without her.

"You're sure he hasn't changed his mind?" Lindsay pressed.

"He—he said he doesn't want our relationship to end after the wedding."

Lindsay's brows shot to her hairline. "But that's huge!"

"It's not—he said we're good together..." Aware of Hannah on the other side of the curtain, she mouthed, "As in—in bed."

An impish smile played around her friend's lips. "And are you?"

"Not helping!"

"Look, Rory." Turning serious, Lindsay said, "I can only imagine how Jamison had to bury all his feelings, all his emotions simply to get through a single day when Hannah was missing. And considering how long she was gone, that's digging pretty deep."

Rory's heart hurt for all he had gone through. "I know."

"So how close do you think you have to get for a man whose feelings are buried that far down to admit he needs you—even a little?"

Chapter Fifteen

"Last chance, man," Ryder warned. "Speak now or forever hold your peace."

The groomsmen had gathered in a small room at the back of the hotel to get ready for the ceremony. Standing in front of the full-length mirror, Ryder was straightening his bow tie for the tenth time. Jamison might have thought his friend was nervous if not for the huge grin on the other man's face. "Still don't know why we couldn't have gone with clip-ons."

"Leave the stupid thing alone, will you? It's fine. And the only speaking I'll be doing is when I give the best man's toast."

"I'm not talking about that. I'm talking about...her." Ryder tipped his head to the right, and Jamison felt his heart jump to his throat, pressing against his own too-tight tie.

Rory had slipped in the back. Like at the previous wedding, her dress was simple, understated, a sleeveless beige-colored sheath she probably thought would help her fade into the background. As if that could ever be possible.

She smiled at Robbie, giving the boy a high five when he showed her the rings carefully tied to the pillow he would carry. She adjusted Drew's bow tie, helped Bryce with a cuff link and made Lindsay's and Ryder's fathers laugh at something she said.

It was ridiculous to feel jealous, but he was. Of all of them. Of the ease and laughter they were sharing with Rory. An ease that had gone out of their relationship as the tension of a ticking clock marked each moment they were together.

"No hard feelings, right?" Ryder mocked after taking one look at whatever was written on his face.

"I told her I'd changed my mind." But he knew now what he'd only started to figure out then. It wasn't his mind Rory needed him to change.

Seeming to come to the same conclusion, Ryder reached over and gave the back of his head a light tap. "Did you tell her you love her?"

From the very beginning, from the first moment they met, Rory had told him she was a woman who lived and breathed love, romance and happily-ever-after. Little wonder she'd turned his half-baked, half-assed offer down.

Never settle for less.

Maybe his mother had had one thing right after all. And maybe it wasn't too late to grab hold of more.

"One final touch!" Rory announced as she faced the groomsmen. They all looked so handsome, from Robbie to his grandfathers, but Jamison... She didn't know if her heart could take seeing him so suave, so stunning, so *San Francisco.*

If Hannah had changed into a girl Rory hardly recognized, well this—this was a man she didn't know. The other groomsmen looked somewhat uncomfortable in the formal wear, clothes that didn't quite fit despite quality tailoring. But Jamison... The tuxedo suited him, and why not? This was who he was. Jamison Porter, hotshot corporate lawyer.

Her hands trembled as she reached for the white florist's box. The pair who had brought the flowers were putting the final touches on the centerpieces in the ballroom and had asked if she might deliver the boutonnieres. She handed out a single burgundy rosebud to each of them, leaving Jamison for last.

He caught her wrist as she reached out to hand him the flower. "I think I could use some help."

Ryder muttered, "You got that right," as the groom turned toward the mirror, but the words hardly registered. Her pulse pounded in her ears as Jamison's fingers stroked the underside of her arm.

You can do this, Rory. It's part of the job.

The pep talk didn't steady her nerves, but it was enough to jolt her into action. She slid her fingers beneath the lapel, doing her best to ignore the strength of his chest against her knuckles, the body heat transferred to the smooth fabric.

"We need to talk."

She shook her head. "Not a good idea when I'm pointing a sharp instrument at your heart."

His chuckle vibrated against her fingers as she finally, finally slid the pearl-tipped pin into place. "After," he qualified. "Tonight."

It would have to be tonight. Because there wouldn't be any *after* tomorrow.

Rory didn't know how she made it through the wedding. Hannah was the perfect little flower girl, practically skipping down the lace runner toward the gazebo, tossing the petals up in the air and then giggling as they rained down over her. The guests laughed along with her only to fall reverently silent as Lindsay stepped into view.

She was a beautiful bride, but it was the love shining on her face that was truly breathtaking. And Ryder—the groom had laughed and joked his way through the rehearsal dinner the night before, but this time he was the one Jamison had to hand a handkerchief to as Lindsay walked down the aisle.

Rory couldn't meet Jamison's gaze, not if she had any hope of smiling her way through the ceremony. She'd told the truth when she said she always cried at weddings, and if the tears streaming down her face when the couple spoke the words *to have and to hold from this day forward* weren't tears of joy, well, no one else had to know.

"Did you see me, Miss Rory? Did you see me throw the flowers?"

Rory managed a genuine smile as Hannah raced into the ballroom, darting between the white-covered tables and fancifully dressed wedding guests. She'd been double-checking with the band, the servers and the bartender while the bridal party finished with the pictures. Everything was running smoothly, something Rory normally appreciated, but tonight, she could have used a minor emergency. Something to get her mind off the best man.

She wanted to believe Lindsay could be right, that Jamison cared for her more than he was able to admit. But she was afraid of fooling herself again, of building another relationship on a lie—this time one of her own making.

Bending down, she scooped Hannah into a hug and spun her around. "You were the best flower girl ever! I am so proud of you."

As Rory set her back on the ground, the little girl

reached up to touch the crown of flowers circling her blond curls. Her eyes were wide as she said, "There were *lots* of people!"

They'd talked about that at the rehearsal dinner. How the empty chairs would be filled with wedding guests watching her walk down the aisle. "Was that scary?"

"Kinda scary. But then I saw my daddy waiting for me, and I wasn't scareded anymore."

Rory wasn't sure what made her turn at that moment, but as she did, Jamison walked through the ballroom's carved double doors. His chestnut hair gleamed in the wall sconces' warm lighting, and she knew the instant he spotted them. The joy, the anticipation…

How many times had she seen it before—on the face of a groom waiting for his bride? Nerves trembled in her stomach, and Rory wrapped her arms around her waist. Not trying to still the overwhelming, frightening emotions swelling up inside her, but embracing them instead.

Jamison was waiting for her…and maybe she didn't have to be afraid anymore.

Hillcrest House's dark-paneled ballroom was decked out in all its finery for the reception. White tablecloths covered a dozen or so round tables. Each chair had a large bow tied at the back. Burgundy and cream roses sparkled in cut-glass vases beneath the crystal chandelier, and a matching garland draped the front of the band's raised platform stage, the cash bar and the tables offering a mix of appetizers and crudités.

But for all the romantic touches and tasteful decorations, he could see only Rory. She might as well have been the only woman in the room. The only woman in the world. The only woman for him…

Their gazes locked, and even from across the room he

could see a slight shudder shook her slender body at the powerful impact.

That's it. You can do it. One foot in front of the other.

But this time it wasn't Hannah who needed the silent encouragement. He wove his way through the round tables and milled with wedding guests, his heart thundering in his chest. Past a growing collection of brightly wrapped wedding gifts, past the towering three-tiered wedding cake, past the photographer setting up to capture the moment when Lindsay and Ryder walked into the room as husband and wife...

So focused on the beautiful wedding coordinator, he barely heard his name over the romantic ballad being played by the band.

"Jamison!"

But when a hand clamped down on his shoulder, he turned and did a quick double take, hardly believing what he was seeing. "Louisa? Greg?" He stared at his in-laws. "What the—what are you doing here?"

His beefy, sterling-haired father-in-law blustered about missing Hannah and wanting to see their little flower girl. Jamison raised a brow at his mother-in-law, wanting to know the real story.

Blonde and trim with classic features she had passed down to her daughter and granddaughter, Louisa lifted her chin. "We want to make sure Hannah is being properly cared for while she's here."

"Properly—is this because she got sick at the rodeo? Good Lord, Louisa! Hannah is fine! See for yourself."

Waving a hand toward his daughter, he expected Louisa's rigid stance to loosen once she spotted her granddaughter. Instead, the woman froze, her expression icing over until Jamison half expected her to shatter. He followed her chilly gaze, his own reaction completely different as he saw Hannah and Rory together.

Standing on the edge of the parquet dance floor, Rory held Hannah's hand overhead as the little girl spun around, making her full skirts flare out from her skinny legs. Their combined laughter rippled through the elegant ballroom, washing over him like a warm wave.

"I take it that's your wedding coordinator."

"That's Rory McClaren, yes." Jamison sighed, trying to hold on to his patience.

She's lost her daughter. It can't be easy for her to see Hannah so happy with a woman who isn't her mother, who isn't Monica.

Rubbing his forehead, he said, "I still can't believe you came all this way when we'll be home on Monday."

"That isn't what Hannah said."

"What?"

"She said you didn't want to say goodbye."

Jamison swallowed a curse. Clearly he needed to pay more attention to the conversations his daughter was having with her grandparents. Maybe he shouldn't have been surprised by his mother-in-law's overreaction, but he wouldn't have expected Greg to go along with it. "And you came all this way because of that?"

"So are you saying it's not true? That you're not planning to come back?"

"My plans are none of your business."

"You're a fool, Jamison Porter."

"Excuse me?"

"You've been here just over two weeks, and you've already let that woman get her hooks into you. Worse, you let her get to you through your daughter."

"Now, Louisa—"

"Don't!" She raised a silencing hand, and her husband

took a step back as if to avoid the blow. "This has to be said."

"No, it doesn't." Steel undercut Jamison's words as he stepped closer and lowered his voice. "If you're here for Hannah, that's fine. But my relationship with Rory is my business. You don't know her—"

"Oh, and you do? Did you know the hotel is losing money and that one of those massive hotel chains has made an offer to buy it?"

Jamison glanced at his father-in-law, who merely shrugged. "Word gets around."

"Right. Probably something you heard at the club," he added sarcastically. "Even if that is true, it doesn't have anything to do with me and Rory."

"Oh, really. So you don't think she'd be interested in a wealthy lawyer who could save her family business?"

"She isn't like that."

"This isn't even the first time she's latched onto a rich man. Did you know that? She went after her boss's son at her last job."

Jamison swore under his breath. "Yes, she told me, Louisa, but who the hell told you? You have no right—"

"I have every right where my granddaughter is concerned!"

"Nana! Papa!" Hannah's happy voice bubbled over the harsh whispers, and Jamison forced himself to take a deep breath and a step back as she rushed over. "Look, Miss Rory, it's my nana and papa!"

Rory laughed as Hannah tugged her over toward the older couple. She looked so happy, so beautiful. He wished for a way to warn her Louisa was on the warpath.

Louisa was wrong about Rory. He was sure of it. He trusted Rory. He trusted her with his daughter. He trusted

her with his heart. He couldn't be so wrong about her...
couldn't be so wrong a second time.

"Welcome to Hillcrest House," Rory said as Greg lifted
his granddaughter for a kiss. "Hannah has told me a lot
about you."

Louisa's greeting was less exuberant, patting Hannah on
the back as the little girl leaned over for a hug. "Yes, well,
our granddaughter has had quite a bit to say about you, too."

Picking up on the tension, Rory crossed an arm over her
chest as she fingered the pendant she was wearing. "All
good, I hope," she said with a tentative smile.

"Hannah, my girl, why don't we go take a look at that
big ol' wedding cake?" Greg suggested, leaving a heavy
silence behind as he and Hannah walked away.

"It's funny how small the world can be sometimes,"
Louisa stated, but Jamison knew he wouldn't find any-
thing amusing in what she had to say. "I used to live in
LA, and it turns out we have a mutual acquaintance—the
Van Meters. You know them, don't you, Ms. McClaren?"

Rory went pale, the color leaching from her face, as she
took a stumbling step backward.

"In fact," Louisa continued, "the Van Meters hired the
company you used to work for to stage their house. Jo-
hanna Van Meter has wonderful taste. She was devastated
to realize some of her priceless antiques had been stolen."

Ignoring the uneasy feeling worming its way through
his stomach, Jamison demanded, "Louisa, what are you
talking about?"

"Ms. McClaren knows. Would you like to tell him...
or should I?"

This was a nightmare. It had to be. Standing in front
of Jamison as his mother-in-law blamed her for stealing
from the Van Meters.

This couldn't be happening and yet—

Rory had to swallow a burst of hysterical laughter. God, Louisa Stilton even bore a slight resemblance to Pamela Worthington. And the look of disdain—well, that was identical.

"Rory." Jamison grabbed her arm, shaking her from the dreamlike paralysis that, no matter how far or how fast she ran, she could never escape. "Tell me this isn't true."

He loomed over her, a commanding presence in the dark tuxedo he wore so well, and she was struck again that this was the real Jamison Porter. Not the hard-body handyman with paint splattered on his jeans and T-shirt. Not the tortured soul who'd made love to her by the gazebo. Not the laughing father who'd played hide-and-seek with his daughter. This was Jamison Porter, Esquire—a man of wealth and power and status.

One who suddenly reminded Rory how it felt to be powerless.

"Tell me!"

Shock had wiped all reaction from his expression as Louisa spit out her accusations, but now Rory could see the emotion creeping back in. She could see the questions; she could see the doubt.

Trust me, she silently pleaded. *Believe me... Love me.*

But he'd never said the words. She wanted forever, and he wanted a weekend. A holiday. A fairy tale...

But this was one without a happy ending. "What do you want me to say, Jamison? That it's all true? That thousands of dollars' worth of belongings disappeared from a house I staged? That I was fired when pictures, receipts, transactions from online auctions were found on my computer at work?"

Tears clogged her throat and burned her eyes. "Fine, I'll tell you. It's true. It's all true."

* * *

"Go ahead and say it," Rory told her cousin the next morning as she sank into one of the chairs in her office. "I know you want to, and I deserve it."

Evie had pulled Rory out of the lobby on the verge of a breakdown. She'd overheard one of the porters speaking with a new hotel guest as he wheeled a loaded luggage cart past her. "You're lucky we had a family check out early. The Bluebell suite is one of our best…"

The Bluebell…

Gone. Jamison was gone. He'd already left. Without giving her a chance to explain. Without giving her a chance to say she loved him before saying goodbye…

Maybe it wouldn't have mattered. Maybe their relationship was destined to end from the start.

Evie handed her a box of tissues before circling behind the refuge of her desk. "You're right. You deserve to hear this…so here goes." She took a deep breath. "I'm proud of you."

"Yeah, right." Rory pulled out one tissue and then another. "Real proud."

How many times had Evie warned her not to mix business and pleasure? She still hadn't learned the lesson and totally deserved an *I told you so* from her know-better cousin.

"I am. It wasn't that long ago that you and Peter broke up."

"And here I am—" she waved a tissue in surrender "—four months later, stupidly falling in love again."

"Bravely falling in love again." Evie glanced away, swallowed hard and glanced back again. Her professional demeanor dropped away, leaving her looking vulnerable, raw, real… "It's been two years since my engagement, and I haven't had the courage to let a man close since."

"I didn't think you wanted a relationship," Rory

murmured, embarrassed she'd been so caught up in her own troubles that she hadn't seen the loneliness her cousin tried so hard to hide.

Evie gave a short laugh. "It's a lot easier to tell yourself you don't want what you can't have."

"But you could... You're smart, beautiful, sophisticated. Any man would be lucky to have you in his life."

But Evie was already shaking her head. "It doesn't matter whether some guy would or wouldn't get lucky with me. I can't bring myself to put any kind of faith into a relationship, and what guy is going to put up with a woman who doesn't trust him?"

"Maybe one who understands what you've gone through? One who's willing to earn your trust?"

"No one wants to work that hard."

"Someone will. The one man who's worth it will."

Evie shook her head again. "Never mind all that. This isn't about me, anyway. It's about you and the way you never let life get you down. That even after everything that's happened, you still believe in love and romance and happily-ever-after."

This time, it was Rory who shook her head as she wiped the tears from her eyes. "I don't know about that..."

"I do. I know you, and I know you won't let some corporate lawyer jerk change who you are."

"He's not a jerk," Rory murmured. He was the man she loved. The handyman, the lover, the father, even the lawyer—all were different sides of the man she'd fallen in love with.

And maybe Lindsay had been right. Maybe Rory had touched something inside Jamison, but she hadn't reached deep enough. She hadn't been able to grab hold of the trust he'd buried so deeply, and without that...

"See?" Evie announced triumphantly. "You still have

faith in people. That's what makes you so good at your job. I know we don't always see eye to eye, and that sometimes it seems like we're too different to agree on much of anything. But the truth is, your strengths are my weaknesses, and vice versa. And that means if we work together, we're pretty damn unstoppable."

"I had no idea you felt so strongly about the hotel after... everything."

"The truth is, I haven't let myself feel much of anything in a long, long time. But this is where I belong. Where we belong."

Where we belong... "Now if we could get Chance to come back."

"That would be the icing on the wedding cake. But for now, it's just the two of us, and heaven help any guy who gets in our way."

Chapter Sixteen

"Hannah, you need to sit still." Jamison struggled to cling to his patience as he tried to figure out how to keep hold of the brush with one hand, the neon-green rubber band with the other and his squirming daughter with his third, nonexistent hand.

"That's too hard!" The little girl cringed away from the soft-bristled brush as though he held a branding iron to her head. "It hurts!"

"I'm trying not to pull your hair, but you have all these tangles." How was it that every strand of his daughter's blond hair seemed to be tied in knots? How was it that his whole freaking life seemed to be tied into one giant knot since he'd left Clearville?

As if reading his thoughts, Hannah argued, "Rory did it better."

Jamison wished he could convince himself his daughter was simply talking about the uneven, frizzy ponytail springing from the top of her head, but he couldn't. Rory had made everything better.

"We've talked about this, Hannah." And they had. Incessantly in the week since they'd been home.

Hannah's frown and saucer-size pout told him what she thought about that, but like it or not, Jamison gave a final tug to tighten the haphazard ponytail before grabbing his briefcase and Hannah's backpack and ushering her out the door.

"I don't wanna go to school."

"You like school," he reminded her—or maybe he was trying to convince himself—as he belted his daughter into the booster seat in the back of his SUV. "And after school, your grandmother is going to take you for a girls' day out."

Jamison didn't know what that entailed and didn't want to know. He was grateful to his in-laws, he really was. But by giving in and having them watch Hannah in the afternoons, he was playing into Louisa's hands. He might have viewed it as a short-term solution, but he didn't fool himself that she had given up on her long-term plan.

She needs you to fight for *her.*

Rory's voice rang in his memory along with the stricken look on her face at the wedding. She had needed him to fight for her…and he'd failed miserably. She hadn't stolen those items, no matter what the evidence might have said.

And if she'd told him what had happened, if she'd trusted him with what had happened, he would have been prepared for his in-laws' accusations. Instead he'd been blindsided by the secret Rory had kept. And for a moment, when faced with the realization that maybe he didn't know her as well as he thought, that maybe—like with Monica— he didn't know what she was capable of, he'd shut down.

He'd retreated back into the shell that had surrounded him in the final months of his marriage and during the desperate, agonizing weeks when Monica and Hannah were missing.

Somehow, he'd found his way back home, where the familiarity of work waited. Where Hannah had started preschool and where, for a while, Jamison had thought he was going to have to enroll himself after spending the first few sessions seated in a humiliatingly tiny chair beside his daughter, who refused to let him leave.

He'd interviewed almost a dozen nannies, but none of them had been right. None of them had been... Rory. He couldn't see any of them knowing how to turn a boring breakfast into smiley-face oatmeal. He couldn't imagine any of them showing the patience Rory had when Hannah asked her to watch her practice walking down the aisle for the twentieth time. He couldn't picture any of them healing old hurts, breaking through a protective shell, making him feel again...

And that was the real problem. Not that those women couldn't be the nanny Hannah needed, but because they couldn't be the woman *Jamison* needed. The woman he loved.

"I don't want a girls' day with Nana! I want Rory!" Hannah's petulant demand so closely echoed the one in his heart that it was all Jamison could do not to snap at his daughter.

Instead, he finished buckling her in and climbed into the driver's seat. "We can't always have what we want," he muttered under his breath as he jammed the key into the ignition.

Traffic into the city was a tangled mess, with cars locked bumper to bumper on the freeway. Not that that stopped other vehicles from trying to weave through the lanes, cutting off drivers and jamming on their brakes. When a red sports car nearly took off his front bumper while slicing toward one of the exits, Jamison swore and slammed on the horn.

Hannah's scream nearly sent his heart through his throat. "Hannah, what—"

"Don't go, Daddy! Don't go!"

Glancing into the rearview mirror, he saw the tears streaming down Hannah's chubby cheeks. The hysteria in her voice told Jamison this was more than worry about him dropping her off at school.

Taking the same exit as the sports car, he pulled off into the first parking lot he came to. Hannah was still crying when he climbed into the back. Strapped in her booster seat, she reached out, clinging to him as tightly as she could.

"Hannah, honey…" Jamison undid the buckles at her chest and pulled her into his lap. "I'm right here, and I'm not going anywhere."

Another horn blasted from the nearby freeway, and Hannah cringed again. Swearing under his breath, Jamison asked, "Did I scare you when I honked the horn? I'm so sorry, sweetheart."

Her chin tucked against her chest, Jamison could barely make out the words his daughter was saying. "What did you say, Hannah? What was that about Mommy?"

"Mommy was mad on the phone. She said we weren't coming home. Never, ever, ever again."

His fight with Monica… The accident… Jamison had heard the whole thing. How stupid of him not to realize that, sitting in the back seat, *Hannah* had also heard her parents' final, fateful fight. "Oh, Hannah…"

"I tol' her I wanted to go home. I wanted to see you and Nana and Papa. Mommy said I had to stay with her." Tears streamed down her face. "But I told her I didn't want to, so she went to heaven without me."

"Hannah, sweetie. Mommy—Mommy didn't want to leave you." His heart broke at the thought of his little girl thinking her mother had left because of something she'd said, something she'd done. "It was an accident."

The words lifted a weight from his chest, and he sucked in a deep breath. The first he'd taken without the crushing guilt pressing on him since the day he walked into an empty house and realized Hannah and Monica were gone. They'd both made mistakes, but he was lucky. He had the chance to make up for them, while Monica—

"She loved you." The words Rory had spoken that night in the gazebo, words he hadn't been willing to embrace, came back to him. "She loved you so much, and she wanted you to be safe so that you could come back to me and Nana and Papa. Because we missed you."

"Like I miss Mommy?"

"Yeah, like that."

"I don't want you to miss me anymore."

"Neither do I, Hannah."

Not when he'd already missed so much. "What do you say we play hooky today?"

"I don't know that game."

Jamison laughed. "It's a fun game. One where you skip school and I skip work and we have a daddy-daughter day."

"Really? Then what do we do?" Hannah's eyes lit up with hope, and for a moment, Jamison panicked. He didn't know any more about a father-daughter day than he did about a girls' day out.

All you have to do is be there for her.

"We can go to the park and have a picnic. We can color in your coloring books and then watch one of your videos."

"An' have ice cream and popcorn?"

"Maybe ice cream *or* popcorn," he offered, not wanting a repeat of the night at the rodeo. "Does that sound like fun?"

"That sounds like the best! I love you, Daddy."

Breathing the words against his daughter's blond curls, he murmured, "I love you, too, Hannah Banana."

It wouldn't always be so simple. But maybe it wasn't always as hard as he made it out to be. Maybe he did have a chance of making things right...and not just with Hannah.

He'd finished belting Hannah into the booster seat when the sound of his phone ringing jarred him from his hopeful thoughts. His boss's name flashed across the screen, but Jamison didn't immediately reach into the front seat for the device.

"Are you okay now, Hannah?"

His daughter nodded, but even he could see she wasn't as excited as she'd been seconds before. "I bet Miss Rory would like to go on our picnic."

"I bet she would, too."

Slipping back into the driver's seat, Jamison reached for his phone. "Mr. Spears."

"Jamison, good of you to pick up."

He heard the dry reproach in his boss's voice but refused to make excuses. "I'm glad you called. I was about to phone in to let you know I won't be coming in today."

"Jamison—"

"I'm spending the day with my daughter." Catching Hannah's gaze in the rearview mirror, he shot her a wink.

"We're gonna watch a princess movie!" she shouted, and he grinned, not knowing—or caring—if his boss could hear her.

Silence filled the line before the older man commented, "You do realize the partners are going to make a decision about the promotion soon."

"I do."

"You've worked hard for this, Jamison. I'd hate for you

to lose out now when you're so close. I probably shouldn't be telling you this, but you're first in the running."

"Why?"

"Well, we want to let all the candidates know at the same time—"

"No, I mean why am I first? Harris has seniority, and Martinez landed the Langstone account. So why me, Charles?"

"I don't understand what you're asking," Spears said stiffly, but Jamison had a good idea the other man knew exactly why he was asking, just like Jamison knew exactly why the older man wasn't answering.

"You can tell my father-in-law I said thanks but no, thanks."

Jamison didn't wait for his boss's response before ending the call. He didn't know for sure that his father-in-law had influenced his boss's decision and would probably never know, but if he took the promotion, he would always wonder. But it was more than stubborn pride keeping him from accepting, more than a need to know that he'd earned the partnership on his own merit.

Taking the job would be taking a step backward—back to the man he'd been before he and Monica separated, back to the man he'd been before the accident, back to the man he'd been before Rory.

He didn't want to go back. He wanted to go forward, to step toward a future that a few weeks ago, he wouldn't have dreamed was possible.

Jamison paced his office impatiently, his hand tightly gripping the phone as he counted out the rings. "Come on, pick up."

The masculine space with its solid furniture and shelves

lined with law books used to be his sanctuary. But now he saw it for what it was. *His* hidey-hole.

He'd had to wait until Hannah went down for a nap after their impromptu daddy-daughter day to make this call, and he didn't want to wait anymore. Just like he didn't want to hide from his emotions anymore.

"Hi! Hello," he almost shouted out a greeting when he heard the voice on the other end of the line. "It's Jamison Porter, and I need your help."

Silence answered his desperate plea before Evie McClaren asked, "Why exactly would I want to help you, Mr. Porter? You broke my cousin's heart."

His own heart gave a painful jerk at the thought of hurting Rory. "I know. I made a mistake. When my mother-in-law told me what happened—"

"You thought Rory was guilty."

"No! Not really. Not once I had a chance to think about it. But Louisa sprang the information on me, and I was—I was blindsided by it."

The same way he'd been blindsided by Monica. By coming home to find the house empty. To find Monica had left without a word and taken Hannah with her.

"It totally caught me off guard, Evie, and I didn't handle it well. I know I was no better than her ass of an ex, who didn't stand by her—"

"Stand by?" Sharp laughter pierced Jamison's eardrum. "Is that what you think happened? You think Peter didn't come to Rory's defense when she needed him?"

Jamison swallowed, suddenly fearing whatever happened might have been so much worse. "Isn't it?"

"Peter didn't let Rory down. He set her up."

"You mean he—you mean the boss's *son* is the one who stole from their clients? And he framed Rory for it?"

"I don't know if he was framing her or simply covering

his tracks. But all of the proof—the online auctions, the storage shed, the emails—all of it traced back to Rory's computer."

Jamison swore under his breath. "How could he do that to her? When she trusted him—"

Like she trusted you? Like she counted on you to be there for her, to believe in her the way she believed in you from the very beginning?

Sick to his stomach, Jamison sank back into his chair.

"Guys are jerks," Evie said succinctly. "Unfortunately, Rory was so shocked by the accusations, by the evidence planted against her, she didn't realize until later Peter was the only one with that kind of access. And by then, it was too late. Anything she said would have seemed like she was simply trying to throw blame on someone else.

"Rory came here for a fresh start. Instead the stupid rumors followed her, and if that wasn't bad enough, your mother-in-law had to show up—"

Jamison closed his eyes. "I have even more to make up for. So I'll ask again, Evie. Will you help me?"

"What do you need me to do?" she asked, suspicion still underlining her words.

Even so, he felt the first kernel of hope start to sprout. "I'm looking for my very own fairy godmother."

Evie let out a short scoff. "And you called me? Mr. Porter, you must be even more desperate than I thought."

"You have no idea."

"Oh, there you are, Rory." Evie breathed out as she reached Rory's side in the middle of the lobby. "I've been looking everywhere for you."

"Why? What's going on?" Rory had tried to take her cousin's words to heart, to believe her unshakable faith in people and her belief in happily-ever-after were her greatest strengths. But some days she felt like the only news was bad news.

It wasn't easy dealing with so-in-love couples, with helping them make their wedding dreams come true, when her own heart was broken. She knew it wasn't their fault. That they hadn't somehow stolen her happiness and taken it for themselves. But she couldn't help wondering how their relationships seemed to be smooth sailing when falling in love had left her beaten and broken, stranded on the ragged shoals.

Evie rolled her eyes but wouldn't meet her gaze, her attention focused across the lobby. "Oh, you know. The usual. We've got some crazy-in-love guy who wants to plan an over-the-top, surprise proposal for his girlfriend. He's waiting to meet with you at the gazebo to go over all the details."

"A surprise engagement. Well, that could end badly…"

That statement caught Evie's attention, and her cousin turned to meet her gaze. "Stop being so cynical. That's my job. And something tells me this guy has nothing to worry about. So go!"

Great. Just what she didn't want to deal with. A crazy-in-love fiancé-to-be gushing over the woman he loved.

Don't make comparisons, she sternly warned herself. *What you and Jamison had wasn't love. Not really. Not on his part. Which is why you're going to get over him… someday.*

Catching sight of Trisha and her friends huddled near the concierge desk, Rory straightened her shoulders. First things first.

Surprise lit the other woman's eyes when Rory walked toward the clique instead of hurrying by with her head ducked down as if she were invisible. No, worse…as if she were guilty.

Tell me it isn't true, Rory. Tell me!

She'd been so sure he wouldn't believe her. So afraid Jamison saw what they had as some kind of escape from the real world. That his feelings for her weren't strong enough to survive the challenges of everyday life. But the truth was, it wasn't Jamison she hadn't trusted.

"Trisha, I'd like a word with you."

The redhead raised her sculpted eyebrows before glancing at her friends with a smug smile. "I'm kind of on break here."

Rory met their laughter with a smile of her own. "Break's over."

The three other women exchanged startled glances before murmuring their goodbyes and heading off in opposite directions—hopefully to get back to doing their jobs.

Trisha huffed out a breath before demanding, "So what do you want?"

"There have been some rumors going around, rumors that might have been intended to hurt me, but that could end up hurting Hillcrest."

Trisha blanched slightly, as if she hadn't considered the more far-reaching consequences.

"This hotel has been in my family for decades, and I'm not going to let anyone damage its reputation. So if you—" The threat stalled in Rory's throat as Evie's words played through her memory. Her cousin was right. She did still have faith in people. "If you hear anyone spreading those rumors, I'm counting on you to help put a stop to them. You've worked here for years, and the staff looks up to you. I'm sure we won't have any of these problems going forward, will we?"

Trisha blinked. "I, uh—no, no trouble," she agreed, clearly startled by the turn of the conversation. "I'll make sure none of those rumors get spread around."

"Good." Rory sighed with relief. "I'm glad to hear that."

As Trisha hurried away, Rory straightened her shoulders and turned toward the lobby doors. One confrontation over, one more to go.

She'd avoided the gazebo in the week since Jamison left, but she couldn't stay away any longer. Lindsay and Ryder's wedding had brought even more attention to Hillcrest House, and Rory was fielding call after call from couples looking to plan their ceremonies there. More brides would say their vows framed by the elegantly scrolled woodwork.

But not Rory. Not when she couldn't look at the graceful structure without thinking of Jamison... Picturing his sexy smile as he teased her about his abilities. Remembering the thoughtful way he'd included Hannah in the work... Torturing herself with the memory of making love in the moonlight...

Evie was right. Rory wasn't going to give up. She still had faith that she would fall in love again, have a family of her own. But while her cousin admired her ability to get over Peter as quickly as she had, Rory didn't think getting over Jamison would be nearly as easy.

The sun was sinking behind the horizon, painting the sky with a gorgeous pink-and-purple haze and casting a golden glow over the gazebo. The groom-to-be stood with his back to her, one foot on the first step and a hand braced on the railing. His tailored dark suit was a stark, masculine contrast to the delicately carved white spindles.

Rory's heart seized at the sight. How long would it be before she stopped imagining Jamison in every tall, broad-shouldered man she saw?

"Good evening, I'm—" The introduction stuck in her throat as the man turned and the faint rays highlighted his face. "Not imagining things..."

"Hello, Rory."

"What—what are you doing here?" she asked, still unable to believe he was real.

"Didn't Evie tell you?" he asked.

"Yes! I'm meeting a man who's planning to propose to his girlfriend at the gazebo. Which is why I can't do this with you right now. He'll probably be here any minute and—"

A small smile played around Jamison's lips. "What?" Rory demanded.

"He's here."

Throwing her arms up in the air in frustration, she demanded, "Who's here?"

"I'm here, Rory," he told her.

"You—you're—"

"I'm the guy who was an idiot not to trust you, not to fight for you. I'm the guy who couldn't let go of the darkness of the past long enough to see the bright future right in front of him. I'm the guy who never should have left and the guy who will do anything it takes to convince you to forgive him."

Tears flooded her eyes, but Rory quickly brushed them aside. After seven days, she was too starved for the sight of him to let anything get in the way. "Oh," she said softly. "That guy."

"That guy," Jamison agreed. "The one who loves you. I love you, Rory. I love your openness, your faith in people, your willingness to see the best in them. In me, even when I probably didn't deserve it."

Rory blinked again, but nothing could keep the tears from spilling down her cheeks.

"I said it all wrong before, and you were right to turn me down. I don't want a holiday or a weekend. I don't want to reach for a phone when I want to talk to you at night. I want to reach for *you*.

"Evie told me what happened at your last job, but I didn't need her to tell me the whole story. I know you wouldn't have stolen from a client. I know *you*." He shook his head. "I've been miserable since I left, Rory. Even after the partners at the firm offered me the promotion, I wasn't happy."

"You turned the partnership down?"

"Turned the partnership down and turned my resignation in."

Rory's jaw dropped in shock. "You...resigned?"

"The job wasn't right for me, not anymore, and it was never what was best for Hannah."

If Rory had ever had any doubt Jamison deserved all the faith and belief she'd had in him, his words brushed them away as easily—as tenderly—as he brushed away her tears.

"I can't believe you quit."

"Well, fortunately I won't be unemployed for long. Turns out a lawyer over in Redfield is getting ready to retire and is looking to take on a partner."

Rory wasn't sure how much more her heart could take. "You mean you'd move here? To Clearville?"

Jamison shrugged a shoulder as if giving up his life in San Francisco to live in the small town was no big deal. "I'd move wherever you are. I missed you, Rory. Hannah missed you, too." He smiled, but a hint of vulnerability reflected in his sterling gaze. "I realize I've sprung all this on you suddenly, but I'm hoping at least some of it has come as a good surprise."

Realizing she'd been too shocked to do much more than echo what he'd told her, Rory reached up to cup his face in her hands. "Well, there is one problem."

"Yeah, what's that?"

"I came out here because Evie told me a man was looking to propose to the woman he loves…"

Turning his head, Jamison pressed a kiss to her palm before lowering to one knee. Despite what her cousin had told her, Rory still gasped when he pulled a small blue box from his suit pocket. "Rory McClaren, you might not be a princess, and I know you're not a fairy godmother, but Hannah and I think you would make a wonderful stepmother.

"I love you, Rory. In such a short time, you've brought light and laughter back to both of our lives, and if I can spend the rest of my life making you as happy as you've made me over the past few weeks, I'll be the luckiest man alive."

Her heart ready to burst from her chest, Rory sank down in front of him and threw her arms around his neck. "I love you, Jamison Porter, and I can't think of anything that would make me happier than to be your wife and Hannah's stepmother. I've spent my whole life imagining the perfect wedding, but you're the one who's made my dreams come true. You're the best man, the *only* man, for me."

Epilogue

One year later

"That's the fifth time you've looked at your watch in the last ten minutes," Ryder murmured as he adjusted the cuff link on his tuxedo. "Is this my turn to remind you that it's not too late?"

Jamison met his friend's cocky grin with a wry look. "Very funny." And no less than he deserved now that their roles had been reversed. Now that Ryder was the best man and Jamison—

He sucked in a deep breath and ran a finger beneath the starched collar and bow tie. He was the groom.

"So no cold feet?"

No cold anything.

The summer day was perfect for a wedding. The sun shone down on the gleaming white gazebo with only a hint of clouds above, and the scent of roses carried from the garden on the warm breeze. Dozens of chairs lined either side of a lace runner as their friends and family had gathered to celebrate his marriage to Hillcrest House's very own wedding coordinator.

Rory's parents sat in the front row. So, too, somewhat surprisingly, did his parents. And Monica's.

A lot could change in a year.

"I'm not nervous," he insisted. Despite the way the second hand on his watch seemed to move in slow motion and the bow tie threatened to cut off all the air to his lungs, the words were true.

He'd been waiting for this moment—for this woman, for Rory—his entire life. He didn't want to wait anymore.

His heart jumped in his chest as the familiar music began to play, and his wait was over. Oohs and aahs rose from their guests as they caught sight of Hannah, looking like an angel in her lacy white dress, and a huge grin split Jamison's face at the overwhelming rush of emotion he felt for his daughter.

She met his grin with a dimpled smile of her own. A flowered crown perched on her riot of curls was already slightly askew, and a white wicker basket swung from side to side as she skipped down the aisle, remembering to drop a rose petal or two on the way.

The music swelled, and Jamison's breath caught as the guests all rose to their feet. But then at his very first glimpse of Rory in wedding white, the rest of the world fell away.

He'd told her once that he didn't believe in fairy tales, and in a way, that was still true. Because this was no fantasy, no game of pretend, no story that would come to an end on the final page. The emotions pouring through him as Rory climbed the gazebo steps and placed her hand in his were as solid and as real and as lasting as anything he could ever hope to build.

Even if she did *look* like a fairy-tale princess...

Sunlight glittered on the lace and beads, the shimmering white satin hugging her curves. Her skin was as luminous as the pearls around her slender neck, and her dark hair was held back from her beautiful face by a rose-adorned headband.

"Did you see Hannah?" she whispered, her sapphire eyes sparkling, as the minister began his greeting. "She was perfect."

"I knew she would be."

Hannah had been as eager—almost as eager—for this day to arrive as Jamison.

"You did?"

He nodded. "I had faith."

Those were the same words Rory had spoken a year ago, but so much had changed since then. For him and for Hannah. Gone was the shy, fearful girl he'd first brought to Clearville. She'd blossomed beneath Rory's care, growing happy and confident, blooming into, well, the perfect flower girl.

And why not? He and Rory weren't the only couple to be touched by Hillcrest's magic. His daughter had had plenty of practice in the past few months.

So, yes, Jamison had faith. He had hope...

And when he vowed to take this woman to be his bride, when he sealed that promise with a kiss, and when Hannah turned back to the happy crowd, tossed the rest of her bright red rose petals straight up into the air and shouted, "Now we get cake!" Jamison couldn't help but throw his head back and laugh.

He had love.

* * * * *

Don't miss the next installment in
HILLCREST HOUSE,
the new miniseries by Stacy Connelly.

*Photojournalist Chance McClaren has—reluctantly—
taken on the job of wedding photographer at the family
hotel while he recovers from an accident. But when his
pregnant ex arrives in town, he may find himself wanting
to take the biggest risk of all. Especially when he learns
that the child she's carrying is his!*

*Look for
HOW TO BE A BLISSFUL BRIDE
On sale September 2018
Available wherever Harlequin books
and ebooks are sold.*

COMING NEXT MONTH FROM

HARLEQUIN

SPECIAL EDITION

Available March 20, 2018

#2611 FORTUNE'S FAMILY SECRETS
The Fortunes of Texas: The Rulebreakers • by Karen Rose Smith
Nash Fortune Tremont is an undercover detective staying at the Bluebonnet Bed and Breakfast. Little does he know, the woman he's been spilling his secrets to has some of her own. When Cassie's secrets come to light, will their budding relationship survive the lies?

#2612 HER MAN ON THREE RIVERS RANCH
Men of the West • by Stella Bagwell
When widow Katherine O'Dell literally runs into rancher Blake Hollister on the sidewalk, she's not looking for love. She and her son have already come second to a man's career, but Blake is determined to make them his family and prove to Katherine that she'll always be first in his heart.

#2613 THE BABY SWITCH!
The Wyoming Multiples • by Melissa Senate
When Liam Mercer, a wealthy single father, and Shelby Ingalls, a struggling single mother, discover their babies were switched at birth, they marry for convenience...and unexpectedly fall in love!

#2614 A KISS, A DANCE & A DIAMOND
The Cedar River Cowboys • by Helen Lacey
Fifteen years ago, Kieran O'Sullivan shattered Nicola Radici's heart and left town. Now he's back—and if her nephews have their way, wedding bells might be in their future!

#2615 FROM BEST FRIEND TO DADDY
Return to Stonerock • by Jules Bennett
After one night of passion leads to pregnancy, best friends Kate McCoy and Gray Gallagher have to navigate their new relationship and the fact that they each want completely different—and conflicting—things out of life.

#2616 SOLDIER, HANDYMAN, FAMILY MAN
American Heroes • by Lynne Marshall
Mark Delaney has been drifting since returning home from the army. When he meets Laurel Prescott, a widow with three children who's faced struggles of her own, he thinks he might have just found the perfect person to make a fresh start with.

YOU CAN FIND MORE INFORMATION ON UPCOMING HARLEQUIN° TITLES, FREE EXCERPTS AND MORE AT WWW.HARLEQUIN.COM.

HSECNM0318

"Are you going to switch the babies back?"

Shelby froze.

Liam felt momentarily sick.

It was the first time anyone had actually asked that question.

"No, ma'am," Liam said. "I have a better idea."

Shelby glanced at him, questions in her eyes.

"Where is my soup!" Kate's mother called again.

"You go ahead, Kate," Shelby said, stepping out onto the porch. "Thanks for talking to us."

Kate nodded and shut the door behind them.

Liam leaned his head back and he started down the porch steps. "I need about ten cups of coffee or a bottle of scotch."

"I thought I might fall over when she asked about switching the babies back," Shelby said, her face pale, her green eyes troubled. She stared at him. "You said you had a better idea. What is it? I sure need to hear it. Because switching the babies is not an option. Right?"

"Damned straight it's not. Never will be. Shane is your son. Alexander is my son. No matter what. Alexander will also become your son and Shane will also become my son as the days pass and all this sinks in."

"I think so, too," she said. "Right now it's like we can't even process that babies we didn't know until Friday are ours biologically. But as we begin to accept it, I'll start to feel a connection to Alexander. Same with you and Shane."

He nodded. "Exactly. Which is why on the way here, I started thinking about a way to ease us into that, to give us both what we need and want."

She tilted her head, waiting.

He thought he had the perfect solution. The only solution.

"I called the lab running the DNA tests and threw a bucket of money at them to expedite the results. On Monday," he continued, "we will officially know for absolute certain that our babies were switched. Of course we're not going to switch them back. I'd sooner cut off my arm."

"Me, too," Shelby said, staring at him. "So what's your plan?"

"The plan is for us to get married."

Shelby's mouth dropped open. "What? We've been living together for a day. Now we're getting married. Legally wed? Till death do us part?"

Don't miss
THE BABY SWITCH! by Melissa Senate,
available April 2018 wherever
Harlequin® Special Edition books and ebooks are sold.

www.Harlequin.com

THE WORLD IS BETTER WITH

Romance

Harlequin has everything from contemporary, passionate and heartwarming to suspenseful and inspirational stories.

Whatever your mood, we have a romance just for you!

1st

WEATHER

Also by Lee Bennett Hopkins

I Can Read Books®
Surprises
More Surprises
Questions

Picture Books
Best Friends
By Myself
Good Books, Good Times!
Morning, Noon and Nighttime, Too
The Sky Is Full of Song

Books for Middle Grades
Mama and Her Boys
Click, Rumble, Roar

Professional Reading
Pass the Poetry, Please!
Let Them Be Themselves

An I Can Read Book®

WEATHER

Poems selected by

Lee Bennett Hopkins

Pictures by Melanie Hall

HarperTrophy
A Division of HarperCollins*Publishers*

I Can Read Book is a registered trademark of
HarperCollins Publishers.

WEATHER

Text copyright ©1994 by Lee Bennett Hopkins
Illustrations copyright © 1994 by Melanie Hall
Printed in the U.S.A. All rights reserved.

Library of Congress Cataloging-in-Publication Data
Hopkins, Lee Bennett.
 Weather / poems selected by Lee Bennett Hopkins; pictures by
Melanie Hall
  p. cm.—(An I can read book)
 Summary: A collection of poems describing various weather condi-
tions, by authors such as Christina G. Rossetti, Myra Cohn
Livingston, and Aileen Fisher.
 ISBN 0-06-021463-5.— ISBN 0-06-021462-7 (lib. bdg.)
 ISBN 0-06-444191-1 (pbk.)
 1. Weather—Juvenile poetry. 2. Children's poetry, American.
 3. Children's poetry, English. [1. Weather—Poetry. 2. American
poetry—Collections. 3. English poetry—Collections.]
 I. Hall, Melanie, ill. II. Title. III. Series.
PS595.W38H66   1994   92-14913
811.008'036—dc20   CIP
                                                              AC

❖

First Harper Trophy edition, 1995.

To my great-niece
ToniLynn Christine Yavorski
In all kinds of weather!

LBH

To my teacher
Fred Brenner
with great affection

MWH

ACKNOWLEDGMENTS

Thanks are due to the following for permission to reprint the copyrighted materials below:

Curtis Brown, Ltd., for "A Week of Weather" by Lee Bennett Hopkins. Copyright © 1974 by Lee Bennett Hopkins; "Thunder" by Lee Bennett Hopkins. Copyright © 1994 by Lee Bennett Hopkins; "Snowflake Soufflé" from *One Winter Night in August* by X. J. Kennedy. Copyright © 1975 by X. J. Kennedy. All reprinted by permission of Curtis Brown, Ltd.

Farrar, Straus & Giroux, Inc., for "Sun" from *Small Poems* by Valerie Worth. Copyright © 1972 by Valerie Worth. Reprinted by permission of Farrar, Straus Giroux, Inc.

Aileen Fisher for "Looking Out the Window." Used by permission of the author, who controls all rights.

Lillian M. Fisher for "Weather Together." Used by permission of the author, who controls all rights.

Isabel Joshlin Glaser for "On A Summer Day." Used by permission of the author, who controls all rights.

Harcourt Brace & Company for "Fog" from *Chicago Poems* by Carl Sandburg, copyright 1916 by Holt, Rinehart & Winston, Inc., and renewed 1944 by Carl Sandburg; "Grayness" from *Everything Glistens and Everything Sings* by Charlotte Zolotow. Copyright ©1987 by Charlotte Zolotow. Both reprinted by permission of Harcourt Brace & Company.

HarperCollins Publishers for "Icicles" from *Cold Stars and Fireflies: Poems of the Four Seasons* by Barbara Juster Esbensen. Copyright © 1984 by Barbara Juster Esbensen. Reprinted by permission of HarperCollins Publishers.

Margaret Hillert for "Listen." Used by permission of the author, who controls all rights.

SUN

NO~SWEATER SUN

by Beverly McLoughland

Your arms feel new as growing grass
The first No-Sweater sun,
Your legs feel light as rising air
You *have* to run—
And turn a thousand cartwheels round
And sing—
So dizzy with the giddy sun
Of spring.

THE SUN

by Sandra Liatsos

Someone tossed a pancake,

A buttery, buttery pancake.

Someone tossed a pancake

And flipped it up so high,

That now I see the pancake,

The buttery, buttery pancake,

Now I see that pancake

Stuck against the sky.

MISTER SUN

by J. Patrick Lewis

Mister Sun
   Wakes up at dawn,
Puts his golden
   Slippers on,
Climbs the summer
   Sky at noon,
Trading places
   With the moon.

Mister Sun
  Runs away
With the blue tag
  End of day,
Switching off the
  Globe lamplight,
Pulling down the
  Shades of night.

13

ON A SUMMER DAY

by Isabel Joshlin Glaser

Noon's lion-faced sun

shakes out

its orangy mane.

Its tongue

scorches

leaves.

Even the bugs

want

rain.

SUN

by Valerie Worth

The sun

Is a leaping fire

Too hot

To go near,

But it will still

Lie down

In warm yellow squares

On the floor

Like a flat

Quilt, where

The cat can curl

And purr.

AUGUST

by Sandra Liatsos

The desert sun of August

Is shimmering my street

And turning houses into dunes

That glitter in the heat.

One tree is my oasis.

I need the ice cream man!

His truck comes just as slowly

As a camel caravan.

WIND AND CLOUDS

GO WIND

by Lilian Moore

Go wind, blow

Push wind, swoosh.

Shake things

take things

make things

fly.

Ring things

swing things

fling things

high.

Go wind, blow

Push things

wheee.

No, wind, no.

Not me—

not *me.*

21

CLOUDS

by Christina G. Rossetti

White sheep, white sheep,

On a blue hill,

When the wind stops

You all stand still.

When the wind blows

You walk away slow.

White sheep, white sheep,

Where do you go?

FOR KEEPS

by Jean Conder Soule

We had a tug of war today

Old March Wind and I.

He tried to steal my new red kite

That Daddy helped me fly.

He huffed and puffed.

I pulled so hard

And held that string so tight

Old March Wind gave up at last

And let me keep my kite.

THE MARCH WIND

by Anonymous

I come to work as well as play;

I'll tell you what I do;

I whistle all the livelong day,

"Woo-oo-oo-oo! Woo-oo!"

I toss the branches up and down

    And shake them to and fro;

I whirl the leaves in flocks of brown

    And send them high and low.

I strew the twigs upon the ground;

    The frozen earth I sweep;

I blow the children round and round

    And wake the flowers from sleep.

SPILL

by Judith Thurman

the wind scatters

a flock of sparrows—

a handful of small change

spilled suddenly

from the cloud's pocket.

RAIN AND FOG

TO WALK IN WARM RAIN

by David McCord

To walk in warm rain

    And get wetter and wetter!

To do it again—

To walk in warm rain

    Till you drip like a drain.

To walk in warm rain

    And get wetter and wetter.

GRAYNESS

by Charlotte Zolotow

Fog on the river

fog in the trees

gray mist moving

the golden leaves.

32

Willow bending,

dancelike,

long arms trailing

trancelike.

Gray morning

gray light

gray mist

gray night.

from

INSIDE TURTLE'S SHELL

by Joanne Ryder

Rain

bends

the tall grass

making

bridges

for ant.

RAIN

by Myra Cohn Livingston

Summer rain
is soft and cool,
so I go barefoot
in a pool.

But winter rain
is cold, and pours,
so I must watch it
from indoors.

THUNDER

by Lee Bennett Hopkins

Crashing

and

Cracking—

Racing

and

Roaring—

It
whips
through
a cloud.

Why
must
thunder
come
rumbling
this
LOUD?

FOG

by Carl Sandburg

The fog comes
on little cat feet.

It sits looking
over harbor and city
on silent haunches
and then moves on.

SNOW AND ICE

LISTEN

by Margaret Hillert

Scrunch, scrunch, scrunch.

Crunch, crunch, crunch.

Frozen snow and brittle ice

Make a winter sound that's nice

Underneath my stamping feet

And the cars along the street.

Scrunch, scrunch, scrunch.

Crunch, crunch, crunch.

ICICLES

by Barbara Juster Esbensen

Have you tasted icicles

fresh from the edge

of the roof?

Have you let the sharp ice

melt

in your mouth

like cold swords?

The sun plays them
like a glass
xylophone   a crystal
harp.

All day they fall
chiming
into the pockmarked
snow.

LYING ON THINGS

by Dennis Lee

After it snows

I go and lie on things.

I lie on my back

And make snow-angel wings.

I lie on my front

And powder-puff my nose.

I *always* lie on things

Right after it snows.

SNOWFLAKE SOUFFLÉ

by X. J. Kennedy

Snowflake soufflé

Snowflake soufflé

Makes a lip-smacking lunch

On an ice-cold day!

You take seven snowflakes,

You break seven eggs,

And you stir it seven times

With your two hind legs.

Bake it in an igloo,

Throw it on a plate,

And slice off a slice

With a rusty ice-skate.

WINTER MORNING

by Ogden Nash

Winter is the king of showmen,

Turning tree stumps into snow men

And houses into birthday cakes

And spreading sugar over lakes.

Smooth and clean and frosty white

The world looks good enough to bite.

That's the season to be young,

Catching snowflakes on your tongue.

Snow is snowy when it's snowing,

I'm sorry it's slushy when it's going.

WINTER SWEETNESS

by Langston Hughes

This little house is sugar.

Its roof with snow is piled,

And from its tiny window

Peeps a maple-sugar child.

WEATHER TOGETHER

A WEEK OF WEATHER

by Lee Bennett Hopkins

Monday/Muggy-day

Tuesday/Tornado-day

Wednesday/Windy-day

Thursday/Thunder-day

Friday/Foggy-day

Saturday/Soggy-day

Sunday

At last!

SUN

day.

RAIN SONG

by Leland B. Jacobs

Spring rain is pink rain,
  For petals sweet and fair,
Summer rain is rainbow rain,
  With colors everywhere.

The rain of fall is brown rain,
  With leaves that whirl and blow,
And winter rain is white rain,
  But we call it snow.

LOOKING OUT THE WINDOW

by Aileen Fisher

I like it when it shines

on the oaks and pines.

I like it when it snows

and a white wind blows.

I like it when it tinkles

with sprinkles of rain

that crinkle the face

of the windowpane.

UNDERSTANDING

by Myra Cohn Livingston

Sun

and rain

and wind

and storms

and thunder go together.

There has to be a little bit of each

to make the weather.

WEATHER

by Anonymous

Whether the weather be fine,

Or whether the weather be not,

Whether the weather be cold,

Or whether the weather be hot,

We'll weather the weather

Whatever the weather

Whether we like it or not.

WEATHER TOGETHER

by Lillian M. Fisher

There are holes in the clouds
  where the sun peeks through,
Patches of sky,
  scraps of blue.
It's raining rain
  and bits of ice
Bounce down like
  tiny grains of rice.

This weather together

changes by the minute

And I can hardly wait

to walk out in it!

INDEX OF AUTHORS AND TITLES